MR. DARCY GOES TO BRIGHTON

A PRIDE AND PREJUDICE VARIATION NOVELLA

BELLA BREEN

Editing: Ranting Raven Editing

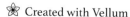 Created with Vellum

ALSO BY BELLA BREEN

The Poison Series

Pride and Prejudice and Poison Book 1

Elizabeth suddenly falls ill after Lady Catherine's unexpected visit...

Pride and Prejudice and Secrets Book 2

Just when Elizabeth thought the danger was over...

Standalone Stories

Forced to Marry

Forced to marry...even though they hate each other.

The Rescue of Elizabeth Bennet

Elizabeth will marry Mr. Collins even if Mrs. Bennet has to drag her to the altar.

Love Unmasked

Is Mr. Darcy Too Late?

Mr. Darcy Goes to Brighton

An Unexpected Second Chance...But Will Lydia ruin it?

Four Months to Wed

An epidemic. A forced marriage. Can love bloom?

Boxed Set

Join the mailing list to get notified when chapters of works in progress are posted!

Bella Breen's Facebook

If you enjoyed the story I hope you'll consider leaving a review. Reviews are vital to any author's career, and I would be extremely thankful and appreciative if you'd consider writing one for me.

Would you like a free Pride and Prejudice cross stitch pattern I created? It's the most loved quote from the book. Download it for free from the file section of https://www.facebook.com/groups/prideandprejudicevariations/

Will you join me for the next book? Follow along as I write at www.bellabreen.com.

Mr. Darcy breathed in the salty, fresh air and sighed. He relaxed against the carriage seat and smiled. He would have a lad's holiday with not even a modicum of distress. Even though this journey to Brighton had taken several days, he was contented that he had listened to his cousin.

He had originally been surprised at the invitation to join Col. Fitzwilliam in Brighton for a holiday, as his cousin had never invited him on a holiday before and most officers took their leave far from their current post. But the more he avoided Miss Bingley's machinations, and the more Elizabeth's boorish refusal of his marriage proposal tormented him, the more he realized his cousin was a brilliant man.

The only concern he had was leaving his younger sister. But he had to escape from Miss Bingley, or he would do something wholly ungentlemanly and demand her to leave Pemberley, which would insult his friend. So instead of ordering them to leave, Mr. Darcy left himself, thereby forcing the Bingleys to leave by consequence. This actually pleased his sister Georgiana, as she did not admire Miss Bingley's false cheer concerning her.

He verily should have been more commanding at letting Miss Bingley know his thoughts about her. The last night he had spent with the Bingleys, she had conveniently forgotten what door led to her bedchamber. His valet had been in the room undressing him, otherwise he would have been well and truly caught in the parson's mousetrap.

Mr. Darcy had departed the next day for Brighton.

He turned his head to look out the carriage window. Pairs and groupings strolled along the Steyne, the principal street in Brighton. According to his cousin, walking on the Steyne was a popular pastime. Mr. Darcy hoped his reply in the affirmative had reached Col. Fitzwilliam by now. He had replied to his cousin's invitation the morning he departed Pemberley, as he had not made his decision until the night before. Or should he say Miss Bingley had made the decision for him?

His lips tipped up. This was exactly what he needed. He would be refreshed by the sea, away from Miss Bingley, and he would get his mind off Elizabeth Bennet. Every time Miss Bingley fawned over him, he wished Elizabeth was in her place. Every time he saw happy couples, he wished they were he and Elizabeth. He had to master his thoughts regarding her, or he would end up in Bedlam.

Brighton would not have been a destination he would have chosen, as it did not have the best reputation. This was due no doubt to the Prince Regent holding court with his mistress at the Marine Pavilion after having abandoned his wife in London. However, there was a military camp located there, to prevent Napoleon from landing, and as that was his cousin's location for the time being, he was more than willing to get away to Brighton.

ELIZABETH ALMOST LEANED out of the carriage

window as they rode through Brighton, so excited she was to view the sights. This would be her first time seeing the English Channel, or any sea, and she was quite exhilarated. She had read descriptions of the sea in books, but there was no substitute for encountering it herself. After that, she did not care what attractions they visited.

Their journey to Brighton had come about principally due to Mr. Darcy. Elizabeth had never forgotten what he had said about the conduct of her family. When Lydia had received an invitation to accompany Col. Forster's wife as her particular companion in Brighton, Elizabeth had known she had to stop her sister from going. Lydia, an unabashed flirt let loose in a military camp with her friend, who was only two years the elder, was a means for disaster.

However, her discussion with Mr. Bennet regarding Lydia staying home had come to no avail, and Lydia had cheerfully departed for Brighton.

Then the Gardiners had arrived to take Elizabeth on their excursion through Derbyshire. When Elizabeth had mentioned her concerns, both Gardiners had agreed and were quite anxious. They had changed their destination in the hope that they could keep Lydia in check. Otherwise, all three had feared Lydia would cause a scandal and ruin the reputation of the entire family.

During the short journey from Longbourn, Elizabeth had often reflected upon Mr. Darcy's horrible proposal, chiefly his thoughts regarding the want of propriety by her family. He had been absolutely correct. It had hurt to admit that even after explaining how Lydia would behave in Brighton, her father had swept aside her concerns.

Along with that embarrassment was the knowledge that she had been so inordinately wrong with what she had accused him of regarding Mr. Wickham. She could not imagine how furious Mr. Darcy must have been. Elizabeth knew she would never see him again and could not write him an apology, but she still vowed to improve the conduct of her family however she could. That included her own tendency to judge without knowing all the facts. She owed Mr. Darcy no less after being so abominably rude to him.

Elizabeth sighed.

"Lizzy, that is the fourth time you have sighed in the last hour. What is concerning you?" Mrs. Gardiner leaned towards Elizabeth, who sat on the carriage bench across from the Gardiners.

She pasted on a smile and turned to her favorite

aunt. "I apologize. I did not notice I had sighed so often." She hoped that would console her aunt as Elizabeth did not want to tell her the reason. No, only Jane knew how rudely she had spurned Mr. Darcy and how mistaken she had been regarding Mr. Wickham.

"I do not know what is resting heavy on your mind, besides Lydia's prospects for impropriety. But rest assured, we will soon have her under guidance."

"Yes indeed," said Mr. Gardiner. "The brisk air off the sea cures all ailments, I like to say."

Elizabeth smiled at the both of them, full of gratitude that they had listened and agreed with her concerns regarding Lydia. It was too late this day to call upon the Forsters, but on the morrow, they would, and she could relax. Plus, with all the new sights and entertainments in Brighton, Mr. Darcy would be replaced in her thoughts. That would give her relief for the first time since she had returned from Hunsford.

2

M r. Darcy took a drink of his hot coffee but paused in the act due to the knock at the door. His valet Mr. Bannerman answered it.

"Hello Mr. Bannerman, have you thrown my cousin out of bed yet?"

His valet turned down his lips and looked at Mr. Darcy, who nodded his head. Mr. Bannerman opened the door and stepped aside, letting Col. Fitzwilliam, who tipped his hat at the valet, into the room.

"I do not know why you persist in annoying my valet, Richard." Mr. Darcy set his coffee cup back down on the small dining table in his room. "Sit down and have breakfast with me."

Col. Fitzwilliam pulled out a chair and sat, resting his right foot on his other leg. "I knew if I came early enough you would invite me to breakfast. Please do order me a plate and make it double everything you have got."

Mr. Darcy paused in the act of cutting a sausage and glanced at his cousin. "Double? Do they not feed you at camp?"

"They do, but I am not sure that what they serve should actually be considered edible. At least for people." His cousin took a scone, covered it with butter, and bit into it with a pleasant sound.

Mr. Darcy nodded at his valet to put in another order for a breakfast plate. If his valet did not hurry, he was not sure there would be any food left for him to eat with the way Col. Fitzwilliam was eyeing it.

"I must say Fitz, I was quite surprised to receive a letter that you had accepted my invitation to Brighton and were already on your way. Not that I am complaining, but what prompted you to leave so quickly? Were you not with your friends?"

Mr. Darcy finished chewing before he answered. "The machinations of Miss Bingley had grown quite tiresome and bold. If it were not for my valet, I would be engaged to that woman."

Col. Fitzwilliam leaned forward. "By cracky, there is a story there for sure. Do tell!"

Mr. Darcy took a fortifying drink of his coffee. "I believe I have mentioned her before?" His cousin nodded with a big grin, at which Mr. Darcy frowned. "I do not know why you enjoy my misery."

"Because your life is more interesting than mine." Col. Fitzwilliam laughed as Mr. Darcy looked heavenward.

Both knew Col. Fitzwilliam's life was far more interesting but that he could not discuss it. His cousin had never outright said he was a spy, but since he could not even roughly speak of what he did in the Army, Mr. Darcy was sure he was involved in espionage.

"There is not much of a story. Miss Bingley nearly caught me the night before I left for Brighton," said Mr. Darcy. "She happened to forget which room was hers and walked into mine."

Col. Fitzwilliam whistled. "Quite daring, that one. She must be far back on the shelf and desperate."

Mr. Darcy glared at his cousin.

"That is not what I meant, and you know it. She is obviously waiting for you and has grown desperate with time. I suggest you find someone for her to marry."

It was not a bad idea, but who could he find that Miss Bingley would accept? He shook his head. "That is not possible. She does not want any man besides me. Therefore no other man would do."

His cousin looked at him with a big grin. "Well then my dear cousin, you must marry so you will be out of her reach."

If he did not like his cousin so much, he would have thrown him out of his room for that statement. As if he would get married to someone he could find in Brighton, of all places, and just to escape the vexatious Miss Bingley. It was preposterous.

"You better eat your food before it grows cold. I would like to see this town that you chatted up so much in your invitation to me."

Col. Fitzwilliam swallowed a mouthful of sausage. "I am so glad you chose to stay at the Castle Tavern. Their food is the best in town."

Mr. Darcy rolled his eyes heavenward again. "Richard, you were the one that made the reservation for me."

Col. Fitzwilliam winked at his cousin as he lifted his coffee cup up to his mouth.

That scoundrel. Mr. Darcy could not help but

smile at his cousin who was so genial and different from himself.

"I think we should start by viewing the camp," said Col. Fitzwilliam, "and its wretched living quarters so that you will take pity on me and invite me to stay with you. Then we can walk down the Steyne with every other visitor to Brighton."

Stay with him? Had his cousin knocked his head lately? "There is not enough room in here for the both of us. You must be daft."

Col. Fitzwilliam finished swallowing his scone. "Well obviously not here, Fitz. But since you are staying for more than two days, you should rent a house."

He sardonically stared at his cousin. "And let me guess, you have just the perfect house chosen already? Completely staffed and room enough for you to stay as well?"

Col. Fitzwilliam swallowed his coffee and laughed. "But of course! How can I not have everything planned? Am I not a colonel?"

Mr. Darcy rolled his eyes heavenward and shook his head. He was not actually displeased with his cousin. On the contrary, he congratulated himself on making the decision to come to Brighton. His cousin was in fine spirits, and this was the perfect way to distract himself from that woman he could not forget, Elizabeth Bennet.

"WELL MY DEAR," said Mr. Gardiner, "what attractions should we take in today?" At the wide-eyed looks from both his niece and wife, he quickly added, "With Lydia, of course."

Elizabeth smiled at her uncle, as they all wished they did not have to watch over Lydia. But they had been unanimous in their concern that she would be involved in a scandal if they did not.

Mrs. Gardiner gazed indulgently at her husband. "I would not mind visiting the pleasure gardens. They sound delightful and have so many flowering plants that cannot grow in town."

Mr. Gardiner turned to Elizabeth. "What of you, Lizzy? I know there must be some places you would like to visit."

Elizabeth smoothed her serviette on her lap. "I am just happy to be along on your trip. I am sure we will have to make concessions for what Lydia wants to visit."

Mrs. Gardiner leaned towards her niece. "That is

where you are wrong, Lizzy. Lydia will have to make concessions for us."

Elizabeth smiled and let out her breath at her aunt's response. "I would like to view the sea that Brighton is so famous for."

Her uncle raised his eyebrows. "You want to sea bathe? Go out in one of those bathing machines?"

"Oh, I believe the sea is much too cold for that," said her aunt.

Elizabeth shook her head. "Oh no, I would just like to walk along the beach."

Mr. Gardiner turned in his chair and looked out the window of the dining room. "The skies do not look bad, so the sea will not be turbulent right now." Mr. Gardiner shifted back to face the table. "It is a perfect day for walking on the beach."

"It is settled then," said her aunt. "We shall go to the camp to collect Lydia and then walk on the beach." She smiled at her niece. "Then, if the day is still nice, we can go to the pleasure gardens."

"Perhaps a stroll down the Steyne if the day gets warm? It is quite fashionable, I understand, for families and couples to stroll down the street. We must do as the locals do, should we not?" Mr. Gardiner asked both women while twitching his eyebrows.

"You just want to stop and have ices." Elizabeth

and her aunt laughed as Mr. Gardiner looked sheepish.

"I cannot help it if they are absolutely delicious."

Elizabeth was quite happy she was with her favorite aunt and uncle on holiday. They would have a wonderful time at the seaside. What a perfect distraction from those thoughts of Mr. Darcy.

3

"I am quite impressed with the camp, Richard. It is much more orderly than I expected." Mr. Darcy eyed the soldiers practicing reloading their Baker rifles as they walked past. The camp was loud with noise coming from every direction. How could anyone think with that continuous commotion?

Col. Fitzwilliam gave him a sardonic look. "You expected it to be dirty and messy, did you not?"

Mr. Darcy glanced his cousin with a raised eyebrow. "War is messy. I did not expect a camp of soldiers to be organized and presentable."

His cousin narrowed his eyes. "These soldiers are."

Mr. Darcy stared at his cousin, whom he was

sure had more to do with the running of this camp than he let on.

Col. Fitzwilliam snorted, and Mr. Darcy turned to look at what had drawn his cousin's attention. A grouping of laughing soldiers had parted to reveal two young women in their midst. They were dressed well, but their behavior was not unlike a light-skirt working.

"They allow doxies in camp?" Mr. Darcy asked.

Col. Fitzwilliam scowled. "Not at all."

His cousin continued to frown and glance at the gathering as they walked to Mr. Darcy's carriage. He was not alone in that behavior. Mr. Darcy was convinced those women looked familiar. It was a ridiculous notion; he had never sought a doxy in his life. But the more he stared, the more he felt he undoubtedly had seen them before.

As the brunette with the long curled hair touched a soldier's shoulder and laughed, it struck him where he had seen her. She was the ill-behaved young woman that had attended the Netherfield ball and Meryton assemblies. Where were her parents or guardian? Who would let such young women alone with a group of soldiers without a guardian?

Mr. Darcy snorted and looked away. They might be gentlewomen or wives of officers and not doxies, but it was not behavior he would expect someone well-bred to exhibit. Never would he allow Georgiana, his sister, to act in such a wanton manner.

"On to pleasanter conversation. Did you tour the town yesterday?"

Mr. Darcy wiped dust off his sleeve from cavalry cantering past. "I did not. After several days' travel, I wanted to go directly to my room at the inn and have a bath."

He glanced over at the soldiers and women again at a loud burst of laughter. He paused in his walk as he recognized one of the soldiers, Mr. Wickham. Mr. Darcy scowled and continued walking to his carriage. Would he never be free from that reprobate?

At that moment, Mr. Wickham turned his head and looked right at him. Mr. Darcy glared and looked away. He had not thought Wickham would be at the same camp as his cousin. Mr. Darcy would rather leave Brighton immediately than be in the same area as Wickham, but he would also not let that blackguard spoil his holiday.

"Your fastidiousness for bathing is absurd. You would have never made it in the Army, cousin. We go for weeks at a time without a bath." Col. Fitzwilliam smiled to lessen the sting.

Mr. Darcy eyed his cousin as he climbed into his carriage. "I can understand why you have not married yet. No woman can stomach the smell of you."

ELIZABETH STEPPED out of their carriage with the help of her uncle. "This camp is much larger than I had expected."

The waiting officer smiled and pushed his shoulders back. "It is indeed a large encampment. Many of the militias have recently arrived. It is the largest military camp on this coast."

Elizabeth grinned, then stood by the Gardiners as her uncle explained to the officer that they had come to call upon Col. Forster and their niece. She gazed around at the few buildings, the busy soldiers, and hundreds upon hundreds of tents.

A strong wind then blew from a new direction, and she covered her nose. Her aunt coughed.

"Oh yes," the officer said and pulled at his coat collar, "the downside of thousands of soldiers in one camp. Well, let me take you to Col. Forster's lodging."

They quickly followed the officer, and Elizabeth dropped her hand, as the stench had lessened. They walked for some time and approached what looked to be the end of the camp.

"We seem to be walking out of camp." Mr. Gardiner turned to the officer.

"Not quite, but close. The officers with families are lodged further back from the main camp to give them privacy."

"That is a nice perquisite. Are their families with the officers?"

"There are children here, but they stay near the family lodgings, as it is not safe to wander around a military camp."

Elizabeth and her aunt glanced at each other. How safe was it for Lydia to wander around camp with Mrs. Forster?

The officer stopped at one of several identical buildings. "The Gardiners are here to see their niece, Miss Lydia Bennet, who is staying with the Forster's."

A young soldier stepped back and welcomed them in. "Col. Forster is inside."

Elizabeth flattened her lips. Did that mean Lydia was not there?

Col. Forster was as genial as ever but did not know his wife's location. "They run hither and yonder, full of laughter and conversation. I have learned it is best to let them go. They always come back in time for supper."

They were soon walking back across the large encampment with their guide. Elizabeth walked next to Mrs. Gardiner, who slowed her walk so there was a short distance between them and the others.

Mrs. Gardiner turned to her niece. "How well did you know Col. and Mrs. Forster when they were stationed in Meryton?"

"I only met them a few times. Mrs. Forster is but two years Lydia's elder." Elizabeth glanced at her aunt.

"I am glad you notified us, Lizzy. I fear Col. Forster is more lax than expected."

Elizabeth nodded. She had been shocked that Col. Forster was not concerned about two young women left free to wander a military camp at will. Mrs. Forster was married, but Lydia was fifteen and obsessed with men. She feared a scandal was bound to happen unless they oversaw Lydia themselves.

As they were crossing the camp, a gathering of soldiers caught their attention. The gathering parted due to soldiers pretending to bow and curtsy as if at a ball, and Elizabeth stood stock still. Her sister and Mrs. Forster were at the center of the group of soldiers.

Mrs. Gardiner gasped, and Mr. Gardiner exclaimed, "Blazes!" They immediately turned towards the gathering. Elizabeth would have died of mortification had she been caught behaving so scandalously. What had Lydia been thinking?

As they drew closer, one of the soldiers glanced at them and then beamed. It was Mr. Wickham. Elizabeth's dread grew as she remembered what Mr. Darcy had written in his letter about Mr. Wickham.

Mr. Wickham bowed and approached them. "Miss Bennet, I am surprised to find you here. Did you follow your sister?"

The Gardiners stopped as Elizabeth was now forced to make introductions to Mr. Wickham with her aunt and uncle. They did not know what a horrible man he was. They only knew what Elizabeth had told them, which was from before she had learned the truth from Mr. Darcy. She felt sick at how delighted the Gardiners were to meet Mr. Wickham.

"Your niece, Miss Lydia, is so delightful and charming. We are lucky she is at camp with us." Mr. Wickham beamed.

"I am glad to hear that." Mr. Gardiner turned to Lydia who was still flirting with the officers. "Lydia, we have come to take you to the beach with us."

Lydia walked towards them with Mrs. Forster in tow. "What are you doing here?"

Elizabeth closed her eyes, but not before seeing the look that Mrs. Forster gave Lydia. It was obvious she had not seen this side of her good friend before.

Mr. Gardiner frowned and cleared his throat. "We have come on a holiday. Now, let us get in the carriage and go to the beach."

Lydia flicked her hand. "Oh, la. I have already seen the sea. The rocks hurt my feet, and the water is much too cold for sea bathing." Lydia turned to Mrs. Forster. "Though we did try, did we not?" They both giggled.

Elizabeth looked at Lydia pointedly, but she continued to whisper and giggle with Mrs. Forster.

Mrs. Forster looked back at them and then faced them and quieted, but Lydia turned away and yelled at one of the soldiers behind her.

"Lydia!" exclaimed both Mrs. Gardiner and Elizabeth.

Mr. Gardiner approached Lydia while addressing Mrs. Forster. "Pardon us, but we must be leaving to see the sights. Come, Lydia."

"But I do not want to go," Lydia pouted. "I am having too much fun here, and I have already seen everything in Brighton there is to see." She tilted her head, twirled her parasol and turned towards the soldiers again.

Elizabeth gasped. Lydia had never behaved so rudely to her uncle before. And in front of Mrs. Forster, too.

Mr. Gardiner grabbed his niece's arm, put it on his and led them towards Elizabeth and her aunt.

Mrs. Forster, who was no longer in high spirits, gave a quick curtsy and fled.

"Well, I guess I have to go now that you scared my friend away." Lydia awkwardly turned around and waved goodbye to the soldiers while Mr. Gardiner led her in the opposite direction.

When they were far enough removed from anyone in hearing distance, Mrs. Gardiner spoke. "Lydia Bennet, you must not behave in such a manner. You are a gentleman's daughter and guest of the Forster's. You must behave with decorum."

"There is nothing wrong with laughing and having fun." Lydia tossed her head.

Elizabeth looked heavenward. She hoped their influence would keep Lydia from exhibiting more scandalous behavior. She bit her lip as she also hoped that Lydia had not already caused a scandal that they did not know of yet.

4

"It is much colder than I expected. Being so far south, I did not expect cold weather at all." Mr. Darcy wished he had brought his greatcoat with him on this holiday. If he planned to spend any more time outside, he would have to buy another one in Brighton.

"You made the mistake many of us did when we heard news of our new station, Brighton." Col. Fitzwilliam kicked a rock off the sidewalk. "Disappointment set in when we found that the water was freezing, the air always chilly, and the sky overcast."

Mr. Darcy glanced at his cousin. "That sounds like classic English weather."

Col. Fitzwilliam snorted. "Exactly."

The tour of Brighton by carriage and walk down

the Steyne had been distracting and a pleasant way to pass the day. However, he had worked up a thirst. "What is the best establishment for tea? I am quite parched."

Col. Fitzwilliam grinned at him. "I can do better than that, Fitz. You have had ices before, have you not? There is an ices stand here that is quite popular. There is always a line, but it is certainly worth the wait."

Mr. Darcy frowned. "Ices? When it is this chilly, and the wind is blowing?"

"The weather does not matter. Ices are delicious at any time." Col. Fitzwilliam tilted his head towards the gathering of people ahead. "See all the young ladies waiting in line? That is another reason to buy ices."

Mr. Darcy shook his head. For all the talk of beautiful women, he had never heard his cousin mention a woman's name. With having to find his own income as a second son, perhaps Col. Fitzwilliam did not plan to marry until he rose higher in the ranks.

They spent their time waiting in line by watching the crowds promenading up and down the Steyne. People were strolling, laughing, smiling and enjoying themselves, quite unlike the hurried pace in town. The atmosphere of seagulls crying, waves crashing, and the smell of saltwater all lent to the holiday air of Brighton.

"How long will the camp be in Brighton, do you think?" He turned to his cousin for an answer, but a movement in the line caught their attention.

A brunette with curled hair leaned out of the line and looked back at them. It was the very same doxy from camp.

Mr. Darcy narrowed his eyes, trying to remember what family in Meryton she belonged to. He wanted to know so he could avoid them completely, if he ever had the misfortune to be in Hertfordshire again.

"What is he doing here?" The brunette scowled as she looked directly at him.

The doxy had spoken loud enough for her words to carry. Mr. Darcy narrowed his eyes.

She had most definitely spoken about him.

It caused others in the line to look back, including someone he recognized immediately.

He stared at Elizabeth Bennet.

Mr. Darcy had thought he would never see her again. He had planned to never enter Hertfordshire county again, specifically because she was there. No man wanted to see the woman that had so rudely spurned his marriage proposal. He did not even know if she had read the letter he had given her in Rosings Park. Would she ignore him? Give him the cut direct?

"Oh!" Elizabeth paled, then a blush formed on her neck and cheeks.

He felt gratification that she was not unaffected by seeing him.

She turned away and spoke to an older couple. Then all three stepped out of line and walked down towards him and his cousin.

"I did not expect to see Miss Bennet again," said Col. Fitzwilliam. "Does she have relatives in Brighton?"

Mr. Darcy shrugged, never taking his eyes off the woman that had haunted him ever since he had last visited Rosings.

Greetings and pleasantries were exchanged.

"I am surprised to find you in Brighton, Miss Bennet," Mr. Darcy said. "Are you here for a holiday? It is a very nice time here, there is much to see. Is your family in good health?" Blazes, if he had not just run his mouth like a young lad seeing his first beautiful woman.

"Yes, my family is well. We are here on holiday." Elizabeth glanced at the older couple with her.

"Good, I am glad to hear that. And your family

is in good health?" Mr. Darcy wanted to close his eyes in mortification. He had already asked her that and she had answered. What must she think of him?

Col. Fitzwilliam coughed.

If he had not been in front of Elizabeth, he would have elbowed his cousin.

Elizabeth gave him a small smile. "Yes, they are in good health."

Mr. Darcy was emboldened by the warmth in her eyes. "Will you introduce me to your friends?" He did not miss the incredulous stare from the woman of his heart. He wanted to puff his chest out and crow that he *could* behave in a more gentlemanlike manner.

Introductions were made and Mr. Darcy hoped his surprise at the properly behaved older couple being related to the Bennets did not show. He focused on her uncle as he needed to win him over if he was to have any hope of getting close to Elizabeth. "Have you fished here yet? I hear the fishing from the pier is quite good."

Mr. Gardiner lit up with delight. "I do love to fish. Thank you for the information about the pier. I may indeed go fishing while we are here."

"How long will you be in Brighton?" He wanted

to cross his fingers that they were staying for longer than just a few days.

"We are visiting my sister Lydia, who is staying with Col. and Mrs. Forster in the military camp."

A movement in the line caught his attention, and the doxy waved to their grouping. His eyebrows rose, as he now knew where he had seen her before. She was Lydia Bennet, the younger sister of Elizabeth. She was no doxy but a gentleman's daughter. No thought came to his mind but this: how could that family produce two well-behaved and amiable daughters and a younger daughter so ill-behaved that he had thought she was a doxy?

ELIZABETH HAD NOT STOPPED WATCHING Mr. Darcy since she had first spotted him in the line thanks to Lydia's exclamation. She noticed the change in his countenance, from geniality to surprise and then a blank mask. Elizabeth glanced behind her and saw Lydia leaning out of the ices line, waving.

She closed her eyes. She had not forgotten what Mr. Darcy had said about the behavior of her family during his horrible proposal. In the time since, Lydia's behavior had only gotten worse. Which was now on full display for Mr. Darcy. After this, she would be lucky if he even acknowledged her.

"Have you had ices before?" Col. Fitzwilliam asked.

Elizabeth smiled, thankful that he would not ignore her family due to Lydia's behavior.

"I have not, but I hear they are good."

Col. Fitzwilliam winked. "You will be in for quite a treat, then. They are one of my favorite desserts, and my cousin's too."

Still wide-eyed from the scandalous wink, she looked at Mr. Darcy, who had not yet recovered his earlier amiable nature.

Her aunt saved the conversation. "I have. We do so enjoy getting ices in town."

"I do not go to town but rarely," said Col. Fitzwilliam, "but when I do, I stay with my cousin here, and we are forever going to get ices from Gunther's."

"Yes indeed," said Mrs. Gardiner. "they do have such good ices. I am hopeful that this will be just as delicious."

"Have you enough time to see the attractions of Brighton?" Mr. Darcy asked. He had not quite recovered, Elizabeth observed, but at least he was speaking to them again.

Mr. Gardiner answered. "We have a leisurely holiday planned, but we do need to leave in a fortnight."

Col. Fitzwilliam smiled. "Now that is what I call the perfect holiday."

"And where are you staying?" For this, Mr. Darcy looked directly at Elizabeth.

She blinked at his directness and ignored the jump of hope in her heart. "We are staying at the New Ship Inn right near the sea."

"That is a nice location. You can hear the sea and seagulls right from your room, I expect."

At his warm gaze, Elizabeth felt heat on her cheeks. Why did her blushing have to appear and give away her thoughts?

"Come back! It is our turn," Lydia yelled.

Elizabeth closed her eyes. Lydia knew they had come to speak to Mr. Darcy. How could she think to behave in this manner? Did she not realize it would make everyone think less of her?

The Gardiners said their goodbyes while Elizabeth looked anywhere but at the man whose opinion she cared for. Her unexpected chance to show Mr. Darcy that she was not as judgmental, and it was completely gone, ruined by Lydia's uncouth behavior.

Mr. Gardiner purchased their ices, and they walked down the Steyne towards the beach, leaving Mr. Darcy and his cousin behind them.

Elizabeth could no longer hold her tongue. "Lydia, you cannot forget your manners as you do at home. You cannot go around behaving like a hoyden just because we are in a different town."

"You are jealous because Mrs. Forster picked me to be her special companion and you do not get to stay in camp with all the officers."

Elizabeth narrowed her eyes and pursed her lips. Lydia was completely without regrets and not the least bit willing to change. She had not thought her sister as bad as this.

"Lydia!" Mr. Gardiner stopped on the sidewalk and grabbed Lydia's arm as she tried to walk past. "Young lady, this has gone on too long. You cannot behave like a child running hither and thither, yelling at people and flirting outrageously. You are the daughter of a gentleman, and you need to behave like it before you bring a scandal down upon your whole family."

Lydia tossed her hair and ate another spoonful of ices.

Elizabeth wished they could take her home from Brighton immediately, but they could not, as she was the companion of Mrs. Forster. Taking her away would cause more scandal than leaving her here. If she could not behave even with their aunt and uncle overseeing her, in no time at all Lydia would be involved in a scandal.

Elizabeth shivered, in part due to the chilled air but mostly due to dread with what the future would hold with Lydia.

5

M r. Darcy had endured the teasing from his cousin the rest of the day and night regarding his obvious attentions to Elizabeth Bennet. He regretted that his cousin was so observant, for Col. Fitzwilliam's preferred method of teasing was to mention how attractive he thought Elizabeth and what a perfect wife she would make. Then he would glance at Mr. Darcy and break out in laughter.

He was regretting his decision to spend time with his cousin. Then again, if he had not come, he would never have run into Elizabeth Bennet again. Who they were presently on their way to call upon.

"Are you sure this is not too early? You only saw them yesterday."

Mr. Darcy turned from the window, enunciating his words. "Yes, I am sure this is perfectly acceptable."

Col. Fitzwilliam laughed. "My word Fitz, you have it bad. I am surprised you have not made an offer for her."

Mr. Darcy quickly turned to the window. He did not want his cousin to guess that he had already made an offer of marriage. In no terms did he want to explain that.

The silence in the carriage unnerved him and did nothing to help ease his stomach. This would be the first time he was purposely making a call on Elizabeth in pursuit of her. Of course, he had to bring his vexatious cousin along.

"I wonder if Miss Bennet has any clothes for the seashore? You know, those dresses that are shorter than usual? Showing a bit of ankle?"

Mr. Darcy turned towards his cousin with a glare.

Col. Fitzwilliam burst out laughing.

"If you were not my preferred cousin, I would throw you out of this carriage in an instant."

That made Col. Fitzwilliam laugh even harder.

"I am not sure you *are* my preferred cousin anymore."

The laughter did not stop until they pulled up in front of the New Ship Inn. Mr. Darcy did not move to depart the carriage until he was sure that Col. Fitzwilliam was over his laughing fit. Then they asked the help to notify the Gardiners that they had called.

"Do you think they have left already this morning to go visit an attraction?"

This question brought to light the same worry he had. Were they even there? Would he have to wait until tonight to see Elizabeth again? He hoped he would see her that night.

They both stood as the Gardiners and Elizabeth entered the room. Mr. Darcy let out a breath that Lydia was not with them. That termagant would try the patience of a saint.

Greetings were exchanged as they sat in the sitting room of the inn. He noticed the Gardiners glanced often at Elizabeth and himself. Elizabeth stared at him with her head tilted to the side.

"I apologize if we called too early. We have not interrupted your plans?"

Elizabeth smiled and the fluttering in his stomach eased. "No, indeed this was the perfect time. We are planning to go to the pleasure gardens later today. I am not sure if we will, as it looks like it will be raining soon."

"It rains often here," said Col. Fitzwilliam.

That started a conversation between Mr. Gardiner and his cousin regarding the weather and shipping. None of which interested Mr. Darcy, but it gave him time to stare unabashed at Elizabeth. He caught her glancing at him then looking back to those conversing about the weather.

He smiled as his stomach eased again. She would not keep glancing and looking away with a blush if she hated him. No, she had to still have feelings for him. His smile grew but then dimmed as he remembered what she had said about him in Hunsford, that he had not behaved in a gentleman-like manner when he had disparaged her family to her face. How could he have been so boorish?

This time when Elizabeth glanced back at him, he was not smiling. Had he been imagining her interest yesterday and today, or was he seeing things because he wanted it so badly? Perhaps Elizabeth was just behaving as a gentlewoman should? Could she be blushing because of mortification that a man she did not care for had called upon her?

The ill feeling in his stomach increased to the

point where he would have to excuse himself soon. His cousin shifted on the sofa next to him, and Mr. Darcy felt the hard end of Col. Fitzwilliam's elbow. He could not do it. It was not in him to make a spectacle of himself in front of the woman and her relatives.

Another elbow in the side, this one much harder convinced him that he had better just ask or he would never hear the end of it from his over reaching cousin. He cleared his throat. "There is an assembly tonight at the Castle Tavern. Will we see you there?"

Mr. Darcy wanted to run out of the inn, jump in the carriage and leave for Pemberley. He sounded like an eager lad begging a woman he fancied to a dance.

Elizabeth glanced at her uncle, who nodded. She looked back at Mr. Darcy with a smile. "Yes, we shall be attending. Are assemblies held often in Brighton?"

He had not expected that answer. So quick was his relief that the fluttering in his stomach threatened to overcome him.

"The Castle Tavern, where my cousin is staying, has an assembly every Thursday," the colonel said.

"The New Ship Inn has an assembly every Monday. At the camp, there is an officer's ball every Saturday."

Mr. Darcy turned to stare at his cousin. If he thought of asking Elizabeth to the officer's ball, there would be words.

"A ball at the camp? I imagine that is a very pretty sight, with all the officers in their regimentals," said Mrs. Gardiner.

Elizabeth glanced sideways at Mrs. Gardiner. Was she fond of an officer in his uniform, just like her mother?

Mr. Darcy stood. He had achieved what he wanted, making sure Elizabeth would be at the assembly tonight. Therefore it was high time for them to leave before Col. Fitzwilliam elbowed him in the side again. Why his cousin took such an interest in his life was beyond him. "I look forward to seeing you tonight."

ELIZABETH WATCHED Mr. Darcy as he left the sitting room. If she had not known him better, she would have thought he had been shy. She turned to her aunt and uncle, only to find them staring at her.

"We have you to thank for this call, Lizzy."

"Yes indeed," said Mr. Gardiner. "You say you met them when you visited your friend in Hunsford?"

Elizabeth willed her blush to go away, but it had not worked when Mr. Darcy and his cousin were in front of her, and it was not working now. "Yes. They were visiting their aunt, Lady Catherine de Bourgh, at Rosings Park, which is next to the Hunsford parsonage where my friend lives with her husband now." She smoothed down her dress. "I am sure they were being polite calling upon someone they knew. Any gentleman would have done so."

Mr. Gardiner's eyebrows rose. "Well, you made quite an impression on them."

Elizabeth felt her cheeks heat even more. She refused to look at her aunt. She was not being singled out or courted!

Mrs. Gardiner thankfully changed the subject. "I did not know they had so many assemblies in one se'ennight."

"And do not forget Saturday with the officer's ball at the camp," said Mr. Gardiner. "I can see why Lydia wanted to accompany her friend to Brighton. So much dancing and fine attractions."

Her aunt nodded. "Speaking of attractions, we

had better start our day if we are going to the assembly tonight."

ELIZABETH HAD NOT BEEN able to eat much of supper. It was ridiculous for her to be so nervous, as she had been around both men before. Except for the fact that one had asked to marry her, she had rudely turned him down, and then she had found out she had accused him of utter falsehoods. And she could not forget his meddling with Jane and Mr. Bingley.

Why did they have to be at Brighton? She was thrilled to see Mr. Darcy again, but she likewise hated it because she was a bundle of nerves.

At least they would not have to force Lydia to accompany them to the assembly. That should help her distress. When they had returned Lydia to the camp after walking the beach and watching the seals, Col. Forster had informed them that they would accompany Lydia to the assembly. Obviously their talk of going to the assembly that evening in front of Col. and Mrs. Forster had prompted them to attend as well.

Elizabeth sighed. Without Mrs. Forster in attendance that day, Lydia had behaved better. How would she behave that night at the assembly with both officers and Lydia's friend?

"You sound as if the world rests on your shoulders, Lizzy."

She turned to face her aunt. "I am worried about Lydia at the assembly. She will have both officers and her friend as an audience."

Her aunt flattened her lips. "I do hope she has taken our admonitions to heart."

Elizabeth raised her eyebrows. "We are speaking of Lydia, my sister?"

Mrs. Gardiner sighed. "You look very nice tonight, Lizzy. Have I told you how much I like that color on you?"

Elizabeth smiled at her aunt. "Yes, I believe you did mention that before." She looked down at her light periwinkle dress. Elizabeth loved the color violet, but this was the closest color she could wear without people thinking she was in half-mourning.

They met Mr. Gardiner in the hallway and walked through the inn.

Mrs. Gardiner looked at her husband. "I do hope that Lydia behaves herself tonight."

Mr. Gardiner squeezed his wife's hand and let go. "I have to think that Col. Forster would not allow his wife, or Lydia, to behave in his company as they do when he is not present. I am sure everything will be fine and we will be able to enjoy ourselves."

Elizabeth hoped for their sake that what he thought would come to pass. Perhaps Lydia would behave herself around Col. Forster?

It was with a lightened spirit that Elizabeth descended from the carriage and walked into the assembly with her aunt and uncle.

The assembly room was on the second floor, and she was sure it rivaled ballrooms in the grandest houses of London. Elizabeth had gazed all around when she saw the many chandeliers, statues on pedestals, and large bouquets.

"It is absolutely beautiful. I especially love all the flowers," said Mrs. Gardiner.

"I agree. The twinkling chandeliers are my favorite," Elizabeth whispered to her aunt. "Who is paying for this? This has to be quite expensive."

Her aunt shook her head, but her uncle leaned over. "Perhaps Prinny has paid for this. You know Brighton is a popular holiday destination for the upper class from town?"

Mrs. Gardiner nodded. "There you are, that is where the money must come from."

Elizabeth nodded, thankful that the cost of

attending the assembly had not been high to pay for all this extravagance. It was an extravagance that outshone even the ball hosted by the Bingleys. She could imagine Miss Bingley's visage on seeing her ball outdone.

She stood with her aunt as her uncle went to retrieve glasses of punch for them. Noise at the entrance suddenly rose, and she turned to see a number of officers walk into the room. Then Col. Forster and Mrs. Forster with Lydia... and Mr. Wickham.

All the happiness and excitement Elizabeth had felt was now gone, dropped into the bottom of her stomach. She wrapped her arms around her waist. She had not seen any attraction between the two of them in Meryton or even in Brighton, when they had found Lydia surrounded by officers.

Why would Lydia be holding onto Mr. Wickham's arm? Hopefully he was not courting her. Lydia had no money and very little dowry, so it made no sense for Mr. Wickham to pursue her.

She sighed. Elizabeth had thought that Lydia's behavior would be better that evening, but that would obviously not be true now. Why did Lydia have to find the most reprehensible, worthless man in the entire regiment to associate with?

Mrs. Gardiner eyed her niece with concern. "Lizzy, are you unwell?"

Elizabeth shook her head and dragged her eyes away from her recalcitrant sister. "I am fine, but I saw Lydia enter with Mr. Wickham."

Her aunt's forehead creased, but she did not say anything.

Elizabeth closed her eyes, then opened them again firm with the resolution that she had to let Mrs. Gardiner know some of the truth about Mr. Wickham.

"Aunt, I have not told you everything about my trip to visit my friend in Hunsford. What I can tell is that I received information from a very good source that Mr. Wickham is not a gentleman."

There, she had gotten it out. She glanced at her aunt to find her frowning.

"You are quite sure? Your letters to us, Lizzy, expressed what a fine gentleman he was with such good manners."

Elizabeth shook her head and hated that had to confront and fix the work of her own doing. "I was in the wrong, aunt."

"Can you tell specifics, details? There are many ways a man might not be a gentleman."

"I can not. I do not want to tell a story that is not mine to tell."

Her aunt reached out and squeezed Elizabeth's hand. "Thank you for telling me." Mrs. Gardiner glanced about the room until she settled on Lydia. "Lydia should be in no danger from Mr. Wickham at an assembly, though, surely?"

Elizabeth turned to look across the room at the gathering of red coats surrounding Lydia and the Forsters. "I do not think so, not as long as they are in public and surrounded by others. But she cannot form an attachment to him. We have to stop that. I cannot tell you what happened, but I could easily see it happening to her, as she is so headstrong."

Elizabeth could not speak anymore, as her voice had broken. This was all her fault. She had not let anyone know what she knew about Mr. Wickham because the militia was leaving Meryton. But now that they all were in Brighton along with headstrong, misbehaving Lydia, she could not stay quiet with her knowledge.

"You are quite worked up about this, Lizzy!"

Elizabeth turned to face her aunt again. "I cannot say any more, as I have been vowed to silence on the matter." She wiped her eyes and composed herself.

Mrs. Gardiner squeezed Elizabeth's arm as Mr. Gardiner arrived with the cups of punch. Her aunt leaned in to whisper something to her uncle, who then nodded and said, "Let us wait for the music to begin."

She turned back to the room but could only focus on Lydia surrounded by officers. This would be her sister's idea of a perfectly good time, but Elizabeth hoped it did not turn into a nightmare.

6

M r. Darcy sat up, straightened his coat, checked his cravat, and pulled down the sleeves of his coat, all to the amusement of his cousin.

"You are fidgeting and as nervous as a man about to be leg shackled."

Mr. Darcy glared at his cousin.

"If you remember, Fitz, you were the one that wanted to call upon Elizabeth and invite her to the assembly. Do not glare at me. I am just enjoying having you in town."

"Hardly," Mr. Darcy rejoined.

Col. Fitzwilliam chuckled.

Mr. Darcy was annoyed by his cousin's continual teasing, but he did not begrudge his cousin's fun.

They did not see each other often, and with the
threat of Napoleon invading this coast, he thought
Col. Fitzwilliam needed all the levity he could get.
Even if it did hit close to home.

They exited the carriage, now having arrived
back at the Castle Tavern Inn, and walked up the
stairs into the assembly room. Mr. Darcy ignored the
decorations and instead looked for Elizabeth. He
had been worried that she would not show, but he
had consoled himself that her aunt and uncle would
not let her avoid the invitation. It was not until he
saw her standing next to her aunt and uncle across
the room that he let out a breath and relaxed.

Mr. Darcy turned to take in the room and found
his cousin staring at him. He raised an eyebrow.

"You are quite fond of her. I have never seen you
act this way about any woman before, Fitz. I am
surprised you have not asked for her hand in
marriage yet."

Mr. Darcy stood stock still so that he would not
give his cousin any notion that he had, indeed,
already done that.

His cousin's eyebrows rose over large eyes. "Oh
you have? And she turned you down?" Now his
cousin frowned and glared at the woman of his
heart, who stood across the assembly room.

Mr. Darcy emptied his punch. He rarely drank spirits, but if any were available, he would have gladly partaken.

Col. Fitzwilliam turned back to him. "If I had known I would have never teased you about her." He studied his cousin. "I am surprised by her answer, though. It does not seem as if she dislikes you."

He did not want to share any details of the worst moment of his life with his far too perceptive cousin. But he also did not want Col. Fitzwilliam treating Elizabeth any differently than he had. Except for his winking. His cousin could certainly stop that. "I asked her when we were at Rosings last."

Col. Fitzwilliam's left eyebrow rose. "You did?"

Mr. Darcy narrowed his eyes as his cousin continued to stare.. "Out with it."

He was in no mood to deal with his cousin's teasing tonight, now that he had been reminded of the worst day of his life by said cousin.

"I did not notice during that visit that she had a tendre for you," said the colonel.

Mr. Darcy snorted. "Well, you could have saved me the embarrassment if you had told me that."

Col. Fitzwilliam opened his mouth, but Mr. Darcy flicked his hand and turned away. He did not want to discuss it anymore. He was quite sure tomorrow he would have to hear his cousin's thoughts on what an idiot he was for pining away after a woman that had already refused his offer of marriage.

He glanced across the room at Elizabeth again. He could not stop admiring her figure, how pleasing she was to gaze upon, how expressive her eyes were, and what a lively manner she had.

"Are you going to stare at her all night? Or are you going to ask her to dance? If you wait too long, she will not have any dances left."

Mr. Darcy scowled as an officer added his name to Elizabeth's dance card. He knew it was unreasonable for him to be angry at anyone who wanted to dance with her, but he was the one that had made sure she was there tonight.

He also did not want to admit that his cousin was right, so he left Col. Fitzwilliam without a word and walked in the direction of Elizabeth.

ELIZABETH COULD NOT BELIEVE how quickly her dance card was filling.

"Your man had better hurry, or there will not be a dance left for him to claim."

Elizabeth felt her cheeks heat as she glanced at her aunt. She did not want to get her hopes up that Mr. Darcy would renew his offer. She wished she could tell her aunt so she would stop making observations like this. But if she mentioned anything, she would end up telling everything, and her aunt and uncle would keep Mr. Darcy away because of what he had said about her family.

"Good evening, Miss Bennet." Elizabeth turned to see the very man standing in front of her. "May I claim a dance with you?"

She curtsied and hated that her cheeks blushed so easily. "You flatter me, Mr. Darcy. I do have a few dances left."

He scrawled quite largely in a dance slot. He then bowed and left quickly as he had arrived.

"That was... sudden."

Mr. and Mrs. Gardiner shared a look with sly smiles.

Elizabeth turned to them. "Do you think he feels obligated to ask me to dance?"

Mr. Gardiner frowned. "With a man like that, I do not think you could get him to do anything he did not want to do."

Elizabeth turned back as another man appeared before her. There were more available men at this assembly than at all the Meryton assemblies combined. This was probably due to Brighton being a much bigger town and a holiday destination.

She was having such a good time dancing that she completely forgot about Lydia. Unfortunately, she was reminded of the Lydia problem when she heard loud laughter from across the room. Elizabeth saw that it was Lydia and Mrs. Forster laughing, surrounded by a group of officers.

After the country reel was over, Elizabeth walked back to the Gardiners. "I am afraid Lydia will cause a scandal if she does not stop behaving like this."

Mr. Gardiner's lips were pursed as he stared across the room at Lydia, who was covering her face with a fan and leaning on Mrs. Forster, whispering in her ear. They both laughed uproariously, drawing the attention of many people with frowns.

Her uncle turned to his wife. "My dear, I think it is time for us to greet Col. and Mrs. Forster."

Elizabeth accompanied them as they walked around the room. Col. Forster was not in the group with his wife and Lydia. He was instead several feet away with older officers. Col. Forster introduced them to the officers near him.

"And how are you finding this town?" Col. Forster asked.

"It is very nice indeed," said Mrs. Gardiner. "We have seen the beach, walked the Steyne, and had ices. We are not entirely sure what attraction to see tomorrow."

Col. Forster smiled. "You must see the pleasure gardens, then." The officers with him all nodded. "They are the finest gardens in this part of England. There are so many flowers and trees that I have never seen before in my life."

Mr. Gardiner glanced at his wife. "How does that sound?"

"I think that sounds very fine. I am quite sure Lydia would love to see it as well."

Col. Forster laughed. "I think if you take one, you will have to take the other. I have not seen them separated since we first arrived."

"Excuse me, Miss Bennet." Elizabeth turned to find Mr. Darcy. "This is our dance."

Elizabeth put her arm on his and walked to take their places. There was no reason for her heart to beat faster or for her to feel tingles from where she touched him. She had to remind herself that it was too late for Mr. Darcy. He had already asked for her hand, and she had turned him down. If only she could get control of her recalcitrant body.

7

Mr. Darcy clenched his fist as he led Elizabeth to the dance area of the floor. He took a deep breath and focused on the large bouquets of flowers that stood taller than the people in front of them. Then he looked up at the large chandeliers glittering with lighted candles. He grasped at anything but looking at the beautiful woman next to him so that he could bring his body under control.

He had not paid attention to the other couples on the floor when he first walked out, but now he noticed that they were not standing in a line, nor were they several feet apart. Thank the deuces that he could function without thinking, but what the devil were they going to dance? It was not a country reel. He could not even remember what dance he had scrawled his name by on Elizabeth's dance card.

It was then Mr. Darcy realized that they were to dance a waltz. He stepped closer to Elizabeth and swore at himself. This would not help him keep his body under control, more likely the complete opposite. How was he going to survive dancing the waltz with her? Their hands touching, his hand on her back, the two of them moving together—

"I believe Brighton is one of the few places where a woman can dance the waltz without first having a voucher from Almack's."

Mr. Darcy looked at Elizabeth and was caught in her eyes. Then he noticed how long her eyelashes were, how pleasing her countenance, how cute her few freckles, how inviting her upturned lips. How had he ever thought he could find someone else to replace her?

He realized he must have been staring at her for at least a minute, but the orchestra started and they took their positions. He held her smaller hand in his with his other hand on her waist and felt her hand on his shoulder. The waltz started, and they were swept away in the music.

The pounding of many feet dancing in unison on the wood dance floor, the smells of the different flowers mingling with the melted candles and perfumes all blended into the background in Mr. Darcy's mind. He focused only on where his body touched hers. He had never danced a waltz and been so aware of his partner's body. He could understand why so many called the waltz scandalous and shocking.

Elizabeth must love dancing the waltz from the way her eyes glittered, and she smiled. She probably thought he was a dunderhead for not speaking. He knew she liked to talk during dances, and he scoured his mind for a topic. "You are enjoying your stay in Brighton?"

Oh good one, Darcy. What a brilliant conversationalist you are.

"I am indeed. We are planning to view the pleasure gardens tomorrow."

He navigated them around other waltzing couples and gazed at Elizabeth again. "I have not seen those yet."

"From what I have heard, they are quite amazing, with plants that grow only in this part of England."

"They are more tropical? Are they native to these grounds, or were they transplanted?" Blazes, Darcy! Small mercies that his cousin was not around to hear his horrible conversation skills.

"I do not know. I hope to find out tomorrow when we go."

"Your younger sister who is here as well, Lydia, will she accompany you?" He wanted to smack himself in the head. Now she would think he was interested in her sister.

Her smile dimmed. "She will. She was invited to Brighton by Mrs. Forster, the wife of Col. Forster. We are hoping to spend time with her."

Why would Elizabeth and her aunt and uncle hope to spend time with a younger sister? A sister she lived with? Perhaps they were here to bring Lydia to heel?

He glanced across the room, where Lydia was surrounded by officers still. Mr. Darcy remembered what he had said to Elizabeth about her sister and frowned. He needed to change the topic before Elizabeth remembered the boorish things he had said.

"Are you planning to see the gardens in the morning or afternoon?"

"I am unsure," said Elizabeth. "I imagine the morning, as the afternoon, from what I have noticed, seems to rain quite often or be windy."

"Yes, it is. I would not want to live here with this weather."

The song came to a close, and Mr. Darcy regretfully withdrew his hand from Elizabeth's waist. He bowed and led her off the floor, back to her aunt and uncle.

ELIZABETH WATCHED Mr. Darcy walk away until he was blocked from her view by the crowd. Even though she had turned down his marriage proposal and he must hate her, she would vow he was still interested in her. She could not forget the way his eyes had held hers while they were dancing. It did not seem like he was unaffected by her...

"How was your dance?"

Elizabeth turned to her aunt. "It was very pleasant." Oh blast. Her cheeks were giving her away again.

Her uncle chuckled. "Well, it must have been pleasant indeed."

Elizabeth blushed even more and frowned at her uncle. "I need refreshment."

"I will come with you. I find myself in need of refreshment as well." Both Mrs. Gardiner and Elizabeth walked over to the refreshment table.

"Such an extravagant setting," said Mrs. Gardiner. "I cannot imagine they do this for every assembly."

"I am thankful for it, though. I was getting tired of the same flavor of punch wherever I went."

Mrs. Gardiner stared at her niece. "So many invitations to assemblies and balls that you have grown tired of the punch?"

Elizabeth chuckled and picked up a cup. She had grown quite thirsty during that last dance. She gazed around the room, as no one had claimed this dance. Unfortunately, that gave her time to see her younger sister waving to Mrs. Forster from her position in the reel. Elizabeth closed her eyes. What were they going to do about her?

"Oh dear, Lydia." Mrs. Gardiner stared at the dance floor as Lydia pantomimed to Mrs. Forster. "Perhaps it is time Mr. Gardiner had a conversation with Col. Forster."

They walked back to where Mr. Gardiner stood with a frown as he also stared at Lydia.

Finally, the torture of watching her youngest sister make a spectacle of herself was over.

"Let us talk to the Forsters," said Mr. Gardiner. "If you could talk to Lydia while I talk to Col. Forster, perhaps we can get her straightened out."

Mrs. Gardiner put her hand in the crook of her husband's arm. "A wise decision, dear. It may be difficult, but between Elizabeth and I, we shall succeed."

Oh no, now she was part of this. Elizabeth forced herself not to look and see if Mr. Darcy saw where she was headed. As she stood near Lydia, still surrounded by officers, she hoped he did not think she approved of Lydia's behavior.

Why did his opinion even matter, though? It was not as if he would offer for her again.

The conversation amongst the soldiers and girls concerned pleasure gardens and caves. Elizabeth frowned upon hearing the caves were in the cliffs at the beach, far away from the pleasure gardens. Well, Lydia would be with them at the pleasure gardens on the morrow and not be able to get into any mischief.

"Mrs. Forster, that is such a lovely dress." Mrs. Gardiner opened the conversation, and the officers stepped aside to allow her and Elizabeth into the circle. Unfortunately, one of those officers happened to be Mr. Wickham.

"Miss Bennet," said Mr. Wickham. "It is good to see you again. I say, the fine air of the seaside must do you good, as I have never seen you looking so beautiful."

The soldiers teased Mr. Wickham, but he did not take his eyes off her, much to her discomfort.

She gave him a small smile. "Thank you."

Elizabeth glanced at her aunt and then back at Mrs. Forster, who had not responded to Mrs. Gardiner's question. "Mrs. Forster, you might not have heard my aunt, but she said you had a lovely dress."

Mrs. Forster gave them a closed smile while she picked at her fan. "I cannot remember where I purchased this. I have so many dresses, and Col. Forster is ever so nice always buying whatever I want."

Lydia whispered to Mrs. Forster, which sent them both giggling.

Mrs. Gardiner tugged at Elizabeth's arm and stepped in front of Lydia. "If I may have a word with you?"

Lydia could not get out of the private conversation, not when she was asked in front of so many witnesses and Mrs. Gardiner being her aunt. She stepped away then turned to face them with a frown. "Why did you have to interrupt me when I was talking to my beaus? Could you not have waited until the morrow?"

"Lydia, your behavior is reflecting poorly on the

Forsters. He is a Colonel in the Army, and they have standards for conduct. I would not want him to be reprimanded for your behavior, as you are their guest."

That was a wise tactic for Mrs. Gardiner because Lydia seemed to actually think about how her behavior might affect others. Something she had probably never done in her entire life.

"Come, let us go back, and you may introduce us to your officers."

Lydia did not pout or fling her hair as Elizabeth had expected. They were correctly introduced to all the officers and learned that a group of them planned to tour the pleasure gardens the next morning as well. Elizabeth relaxed, as she was quite sure Lydia would behave or at least not get into any trouble with a group of officers surrounding her and Mrs. Forster.

Elizabeth and Mrs. Gardiner took their leave and walked to the refreshment table, where Mr. Gardiner was sampling the fruits. "I hope you had a better talk with Lydia, but I cannot imagine so. My talk with Col. Forster did not go as expected. He assured me that girls would be girls, and he was happy that his wife had such a good friend in Lydia."

Elizabeth could easily imagine how a man could

ignore his wife's behavior, or her friend's, as her own father had done the same since she could remember.

"Well, let us hope that my talk with Lydia bears fruit. I think what I said might have gotten through to her."

8

M r. Darcy squinted at the occupants of the carriage driving down the Steyne.

"You are going to ruin your eyes if you keep doing that."

Mr. Darcy ignored his cousin. He also ignored the group of officers milling about as well. He hoped they were not waiting for Elizabeth's younger sister and her friend, the wife of some soldier. He had learned, thanks to Elizabeth's admonition, to not be so judgmental regarding family members. Such as the youngest Bennet's behavior reflecting on the elder sisters. But that did not mean that he tolerated ill behavior when it did occur.

Two carriages pulled up to the pleasure gardens. Elizabeth's aunt and uncle descended first, then Elizabeth. She was cheerful and lively, the force of her beauty and personality struck him again, even though he had just danced with her last night.

He smiled, and his grin grew wider at her warm return of a smile. Even though they were separated by several feet, she with her relatives and he with his, he felt an almost physical connection with her.

He pulled his eyes away from Elizabeth to see the second carriage disgorge the youngest Bennet girl and her friend. The group of soldiers immediately surrounded them. He narrowed his eyes at the prospect of two young women escorted by several soldiers, none of whom was the one woman's husband.

They all started out walking through the gardens as a large group, but with the Gardiners and Elizabeth reading about the different plants from their pamphlets, the younger group of officers with the two young women quickly outstripped them. Col. Fitzwilliam finally did a good turn by walking with Elizabeth's aunt and uncle and pointing out specific attributes or his personal knowledge of the different foliage. That left Elizabeth and himself to walk at their own pace.

"These plants have such bright and lovely flowers. I have seen nothing like it before." Elizabeth gently touched a large yellow flower with red edging.

"You would not see that locally, as it is a tropical flower from the islands in the Caribbean." He stood as close to her as he dared, but still within the boundaries of propriety.

Elizabeth turned to him as they walked to the next grouping of plants. "Have you ever wanted to sail and visit those tropical islands? I would be afraid of the storms and the long voyage. I do not think I would go."

His heartbeat picked up at the thought of Elizabeth lost at sea.

"I have never considered it. I do have the offer at any time of traveling on one of the East India Trading Company's ships to India."

"You do? Did you know one of the owners?"

Mr. Darcy shook his head with a smile. "I have stock. Any stockholder can travel with the ship if they wish."

They stopped in front of a large tree with huge white flowers and a pleasant fragrance. Elizabeth leaned in and sniffed the flower. "Oh, this is lovely. Imagine having this growing outside to enjoy all year round."

"It is possible to grow plants like these even in the north of England and Derbyshire."

Elizabeth turned with a furrowed brow. "You jest."

He smiled at her disbelief. "There are houses constructed entirely of glass. The plants grow inside and are warmed throughout the winter by the sun. They are kept free from the dangers of winter. It is possible to have fresh oranges any time with one of the glass houses."

He was gratified by seeing Elizabeth speechless.

"Pemberley has an orangery such as I described."

Instead of a calculating look or even desire that he had expected, Elizabeth stared down at her hands holding the pleasure garden pamphlet.

"Shall we move on, then?" She led the way to a new grouping of plants, but Mr. Darcy did not pay attention to where they went, as he was stuck on Elizabeth's behavior when he mentioned the orangery at Pemberley.

Elizabeth's cheerful nature quickly reasserted itself and the rest of their tour of the gardens passed without incident. They caught up with her aunt and uncle, who were entertained by Col. Fitzwilliam's stories of his travels and the unusual plants and animals.

"My, look at the time," said Mr. Gardiner. "We must get back to the inn for supper." Mr. Gardiner tucked his pocket watch back in his coat.

Mr. Darcy looked at his and saw it was indeed late. Would it be too forward of him to ask the Gardiners and Elizabeth to dine with him and his cousin at the Castle Tavern Inn? He twisted his lips as he realized that he would have to invite her youngest sister as well. He was not sure he could stomach that termagant, even if it was for Elizabeth.

He spied her friend surrounded by officers approaching their group. Perhaps he would not need to invite Lydia after all? She would probably dine with her friend and husband at the camp. He hoped they had a personal chef because from what Col. Fitzwilliam said, the camp food was abysmal.

"Mrs. Forster," said Mr. Gardiner. "Is Lydia not with you?"

Mr. Darcy eyed the group and realized that Elizabeth's sister was not in their group.

"She is not already here?" The woman looked surprised and confused. "I thought for sure..." She then looked behind her in the group of officers, but they stepped aside, also looking around. It was quite obvious she was indeed missing.

"Where is Lydia?" Elizabeth's voice was shrill, her concern for her sister evident.

Mrs. Forster turned back to their group with a bewildered countenance.

THIS COULD NOT BE. Lydia could not have done something when she knew they had Mr. Darcy and Col. Fitzwilliam in attendance. They had just talked to her about her behavior the night before. If Mr. Darcy had ever actually thought of renewing his proposal, her sister's behavior has surely driven it out of his head.

Mr. Gardiner stepped towards Mrs. Forster. "Tell us what happened."

"Nothing happened, though, I do not think?" She was confused and yet could not meet their eyes.

Elizabeth pursed her lips and clenched her dress to stop from blurting accusations. At least she had learned something from misjudging Mr. Darcy so horribly before.

One of the officers cleared his throat. "There was a time when we were not altogether and had split off into several groups in the gardens."

Mr. Gardiner eyed that man. "Lydia is not alone

then? If they have gotten lost, at least she is with others. And officers know how to find their—"

"There is no one else missing, though." Spoke another officer. "Oh, except for Mr. Wickham, who joined us later."

Elizabeth gasped. Mr. Wickham? She closed her eyes and ran her hand over her forehead.

She did not even want to glance at Mr. Darcy to see the scowl on his countenance. It was as if everything he had said about her family's behavior and Mr. Wickham was playing out during this holiday. She was worried for her sister, of course, yet she was also angry at Lydia. But more than that was an overwhelming sadness, as she knew with a certainty she would never see Mr. Darcy again.

"Mr. Wickham?" queried Mr. Darcy.

"Yes, he joined us later. He said he had been delayed by something."

Elizabeth was sure that was a lie and that he only delayed himself long enough to avoid meeting Mr. Darcy. Now her head hurt, and she rubbed her forehead, seeking relief from all the worries and pain that troubled her.

Search parties were quickly organized from the gathered men. Elizabeth and Mrs. Gardiner stayed near the entrance of the pleasure gardens in case

Lydia found her way back. The sun was setting with a colorful display, but she was too distraught to enjoy it. She wiped her eyes and sniffed.

"Lizzy, it is not like you to suffer from dramatics."

"I am not, aunt." She wiped her nose with a handkerchief. "If only I had told you... but I could not, it was not my story to tell. It would hurt someone... this is all my fault."

"You are not making any sense. Do you have knowledge as to what transpired here tonight?"

Elizabeth sat up and faced her aunt. "I did not tell you all I knew about Mr. Wickham the other day. I found out from a very accurate source that he only has the looks of a gentleman and none of the goodness or morals."

"Oh dear, but that does sound a bit like bad apples."

Elizabeth shook her head. "I cannot tell you the specifics, as if I reveal exactly what happened, it would hurt someone's reputation."

Mrs. Gardiner nodded at her to go on.

"Mr. Wickham has not just preyed upon young women wherever he has been, but has shown the most immoral behavior and spread falsehoods determined to ruin the name of Mr. Darcy."

Mrs. Gardiner's brows furrowed.

"Mr. Darcy corroborated much of what Mr. Wickham said to me, but then matters differed greatly regarding the living at a parsonage. It was willed to Mr. Wickham, but he turned it down and asked for money instead, several thousand pounds. He received it, but then just a few years later, he demanded the living." Elizabeth pursed her , as her aunt had not spoken. "You can ask Col. Fitzwilliam. He knows all the particulars as well."

"My dear, I do not know what to think. They both seem like proper gentleman. You are sure about what you heard about Mr. Wickham?"

Elizabeth nodded. "You will see, aunt. Mr. Darcy is the true gentleman."

9

M r. Darcy stood near his cousin as he organized the officers into groups of search parties. Mr. Darcy hoped they would be found walking down a road in Brighton, or perhaps a road outside of the town, having wandered too far in the caves. It would be much better than being found huddled together underground. Then Elizabeth's sister would have to marry that worthless lout, and Elizabeth would have Wickham as a brother-in-law.

Mr. Darcy did not join in the search. He stayed with his cousin and Mr. Gardiner. He did not leave as he felt this situation was his fault. If only he had made it known that Wickham was a reprobate and scoundrel, then none of what Wickham had done since would have occurred. He would have saved many families much misery. Now, he was present at a situation similar to the one his own sister had faced not that long ago. Except in this case, Lydia had not eloped with Wickham, well, as far as they knew, which was not much.

Col. Fitzwilliam looked at Mr. Gardiner. "Had Miss Lydia shown any signs of partiality to Mr. Wickham?"

"Not that I knew," said Mr. Gardiner. "But we have not been with her at all times since we arrived in Brighton. She has had much time in camp with her friend, Mrs. Forster. Perhaps she did form a tendre for him. I really do not know."

Her uncle looked more angry than worried. He must still have hopes that Lydia had not been ravished by Wickham. Even if she had not been, she had surely been compromised. To be missing with a man—the rumors would destroy her. And in turn, destroy the Bennet family, because scandal afflicting one daughter affected them all.

Mr. Darcy frowned at the ill feeling in his chest. Due to his pride of not revealing difficulties, Elizabeth was now affected by a horrible act Wickham had committed. He was quite sure that lout was behind this. That scoundrel never did anything unless he had completely calculated its return for him in the positive.

He flattened his lips, but there was nothing he could do about the situation now. He would provide monetary assistance but would not actively help search. Frankly, the world would be better off without Wickham ever being found.

The first group of soldiers came back and reported they had found no signs of the missing pair in the gardens. They had even checked behind bushes, said one soldier with a smirk. Col. Fitzwilliam's scowl was so great that the soldier immediately wiped the smirk off his face and straightened up.

"Do not forget that the young woman's uncle is here and quite concerned for his niece." Col. Fitzwilliam was every inch an officer of the great British Army.

Mr. Darcy was impressed. The cousin he saw now could lead thousands into battle, and everyone would follow him on the strength of his personality.

More search parties reported back stating the same thing, no sign of either missing person.

He bit the inside of his cheek. Mr. Darcy hesitated to suggest that they should check the roads out of town. An elopement was uppermost on his mind.

Col. Fitzwilliam knew the entirety of Wickham's dealings with Georgiana, and should he think it necessary to search the roads, he would state it. Mr. Darcy therefore made no suggestion.

Col. Fitzwilliam waved for Mrs. Forster to be brought to him, as she was currently weeping near Mr. Gardiner. "Can you tell me anything? Do you have any idea of where they might have gone? Did they have any plans?"

Mrs. Forster shook her head. "No. We were all together when we went down the well, and then—"

"Well? You went down a well?" Col. Fitzwilliam's lips were so flat you could not even tell he had lips anymore.

Mr. Darcy sighed and looked heavenward. That information would have been useful at the beginning of the search.

Mrs. Forster wiped her face. She looked up and then quickly looked back down at her trembling hands. "We heard soldiers talking of caves in the cliff, and Miss Lydia and I wanted to see what we could find in the caves. Mr. Wickham said there might be treasure down there from smugglers. It would be a fun lark." She sniffed and continued. "So Lydia and I went down first after she threw her candle down. Then Mr. Denny and Mr. Wickham."

Mr. Darcy snorted and shook his head.

"We were all in a group. We were only to walk through the tunnel, but Wickham walked off right away. He went so fast that Lydia ran to catch up with him. I could not even hear or see them anymore, and I yelled, and I kept yelling but never heard them. I asked Mr. Denny to take me back to the ladder. I wanted to get out of there." She wiped her nose with a handkerchief. "I thought maybe they came out another exit and would meet us at the entrance to the gardens."

There were silent for many moments as the men digested the ridiculous story they had just heard. It sounded stupid enough to be true. Mrs. Forster must have been used to being able to do whatever she wanted. He imagined her husband would handle her quite differently after this.

What happened to Wickham, he did not know nor care, but he hoped he got lost down in the caves. It would do the world good to be rid of him. But this would ruin Lydia's reputation and in turn the reputation of the Bennet family unless they could keep the scandal hidden.

Mr. Darcy looked at the soldiers. They might all write home about this, but if none of them were from Hertfordshire, the Bennets might just be able to keep this quiet. But if she had been ravished by Wickham, nothing at all would be able to keep that quiet.

"Well, it is obvious what we need to do," said Mr. Gardiner. "We need to go down into the caves and find them."

"We will need supplies if we are going to go down into the caves," said Col. Fitzwilliam. He detailed a list of what they would need so that no one else would get lost, such as chalk for marking cave walls, lanterns, and rope. A soldier ran back to the camp to alert Col. Forster that Miss Lydia and Mr. Wickham were missing.

Mrs. Forster led them to where the well was located in the garden. Two soldiers stayed near the well and did not go to the entrance of the gardens with the rest of the group.

Mrs. Gardiner and Elizabeth stood as they saw the group of men approaching. They both walked quickly to Mr. Gardiner, but he did not even have to shake his head before they knew that Lydia had not been found. They were both aghast upon hearing that Mrs. Forster and Lydia as well as another soldier and Wickham had gone down a well to explore the caves.

"What were they thinking?" Mrs. Gardiner uncharacteristically blurted out.

"They were not, my dear. That is quite obvious. They probably thought they would have a quick look, not realizing the dangers that could befall them, such as the cave collapsing, the tide rising and flooding the cave, let alone—"

"Collapsing? Flooding?" Elizabeth felt faint. Getting lost in the caves was one thing, but that her sister could be in danger of losing her life or perhaps already... "You must find her! What are they going to do to find her?"

"Now Lizzy, everything will be all right. You will see." Mr. Gardiner put his arm around Elizabeth. The other was already holding Mrs. Gardiner. "Col. Fitzwilliam has everything all organized. I must say, he is a fine example of the British Army. They will be found, and everything will soon be to rights."

Mr. Gardiner's assurances did not make Elizabeth feel any better.

"Excuse me, Miss Bennet."

Elizabeth turned to face Mr. Darcy.

"I am sure you have been wishing my absence to

deal with this unfortunate situation. I shall leave you now." Mr. Darcy bowed and walked to his carriage.

Elizabeth swallowed as she watched him walk away and out of her life. She felt the loss of Mr. Darcy but was angry at him too for not staying to help search for her sister. She turned away from him and looked back at her aunt and uncle.

Her aunt reached out and squeezed Elizabeth's arm. "He knew we would not want him around when Lydia was found. Or that we would not want to keep him entertained while we waited for word of Lydia."

What her aunt said made perfect sense, though she still felt abandoned. Just when she had thought they had grown closer and had hoped that he would... but it was no use to think of it. Lydia's actions had driven Mr. Darcy away, and she would never see him again. It was best for her to focus on the situation at hand.

"What is being done now to find them?"

Mr. Gardiner looked at Elizabeth. "Groups of soldiers will be sent down with candles and lanterns. They will use chalk to mark where they have been and in what direction they went. It is organized very well by Col. Fitzwilliam. I am quite sure they will be found quickly."

Elizabeth flashed a quick smile, but she knew

everything would not be all right. Now that more people had gotten involved in the search, news of this was sure to travel.

The sun had settled under the horizon, and there was no use for Mrs. Gardiner and Elizabeth to be at the pleasure garden anymore. They took their carriage back to the New Ship Inn but did not eat much supper as they did not have much of an appetite. Neither could imagine sleeping when Lydia was lost out there somewhere, so they both went down to the sitting room of the inn and waited for word of Lydia.

10

M r. Darcy traveled back to the Castle Tavern Inn and spoke with the owner. He ordered refreshments and blankets. Mr. Darcy offered the use of his carriage for the Inn to deliver the food, hot beverages and blankets to the men working to find Elizabeth's sister. The owner was much obliged, and platters of sandwiches as well as hot tea were quickly ready to be delivered.

Mr. Darcy was gratified to find that Col. Fitzwilliam had sent soldiers to check the roads traveling out of Brighton. No one was sure how far the caves continued until several of the locals arrived. They had come to help once they knew something was happening in the gardens. The underground cave system went on for miles, they told Col. Fitzwilliam.

"I do not think Miss Lydia would be able to travel that far, though, as she was in a day dress and walking shoes," stated Col. Fitzwilliam to the gathered men. "Mr. Wickham, as a soldier, would be able to walk much farther. If his goal was not to run off with Miss Lydia, but desertion, we may be find her alone somewhere in the cave system."

All search parties that reported in were not sent back out until they had warmed themselves from the hot beverages and blankets. They went back out with those supplies to stay warm as well as for Lydia, if they found her. No one felt like keeping any supplies for Wickham. Sentiment ran high against him for going down in a cave system with an unmarried young woman and getting lost, even though he was a soldier and should have known better.

It had been hours, and they still had not been found yet. Mr. Gardiner had stayed at the pleasure gardens, but it was obvious that it was far past time for him to go back to the inn. Mr. Darcy convinced him to that his wife and niece were probably awake and unable to sleep with worry. It would be much better for the Gardiners if they could sleep and be ready for when Lydia was found.

Mr. Darcy dropped off Mr. Gardiner at the New Ship Inn during one of his runs to the Castle Tavern Inn for more refreshments. He did not go into the inn with Mr. Gardiner because if Elizabeth was awake and waiting downstairs, she would not want him to see her upset. And if she was upstairs sleeping, he had no reason to go into the inn at all.

The local men were invaluable to the search parties, as they knew of some other passages that led to the caves. One man produced a crude map of the cave system along with one other entry point in the town.

Searchers went out in groups of two so that when they found Lydia and if she was alone, she would be kept respectable by having two men with her instead of just one. Therefore, she would not be compromised if she had not already been, by Wickham. Mr. Darcy did not think his cousin's order was foolish, even though the scandal from it could already have ruined her. Col. Fitzwilliam was doing everything he could to ensure that no scandal came from their search efforts to Lydia, though he probably was only concerned about no scandal reaching Elizabeth.

"Fitz, why you are still here?" Col. Fitzwilliam blurted when his cousin appeared suddenly at his side. "There is nothing for you to do, and it is much too dangerous for you to go down in the caves."

Mr. Darcy raised his eyebrows. "Where did you think those sandwiches and hot tea came from? The fairies?"

Col. Fitzwilliam held up a sandwich. "You mean... you have provided this?"

Mr. Darcy lifted one side of his mouth. "Yes. I have been running my carriage back and forth to the Castle Tavern Inn to bring hot beverages, sandwiches, and blankets, and to take away spent soldiers."

Col. Fitzwilliam raised his eyebrows. "Blazes, Fitz! That has to be quite a tidy sum of money you have outlaid."

Mr. Darcy gave him a flat stare. "I can certainly afford it. Besides, I feel it is my duty at the very least, as I did not let anyone in Meryton know about Wickham's true nature."

Col. Fitzwilliam shook his head as he swallowed a bite of sandwich. "It is not your fault. The blame is solely on Wickham's shoulders. When we find that lout... I would not be surprised if he comes back to camp worse for wear."

"I would not gamble on that at all. As a matter of fact, I might even join them."

Col. Fitzwilliam stopped chewing and stared. "You? Pummel Wickham?"

"You of all people should know how much I have wanted to thrash him over his lifetime. This is the perfect opportunity. However, as I am no relation to the missing woman, it would be scandalous if I did give Wickham the thrashing he so deserves."

Col. Fitzwilliam studied his cousin. "You care for her very much, do you not?"

Mr. Darcy looked at him quizzically.

"No, not Miss Lydia. Her sister."

Mr. Darcy looked back at the well where several soldiers were standing waiting for the search teams to report in. "I do like her." He shook his head. "There is nothing to be done about it. You know what happened the last time I offered."

"Do not be a nodcock, Fitz. I could tell she had a fondness for you. I think you might be surprised and find that she has changed her mind about you." Col. Fitzwilliam glanced at his cousin and then focused on the black opening of the well.

Mr. Darcy shook his head and said nothing more.

WHEN MR. GARDINER had walked into the inn, Elizabeth and her aunt had rushed towards him with cries of happiness and hugs. It was not until they stepped back and saw his countenance that their shoulders drooped. Lydia was still missing.

"Are the searches being run well?" asked Mrs. Gardiner. "Do they think they will be able to find her?"

Mr. Gardiner held his wife. "The searches are run in a very proficient manner by Col. Fitzwilliam. He is doing everything I would have done and more. I have no doubt whatsoever that she will be found. He has been very thorough with marking areas that have been searched and employing the search teams with necessary provisions to stay warm and not lost."

Elizabeth smiled yet felt pangs of sadness, as Col. Fitzwilliam was Mr. Darcy's cousin, which reminded her of the man himself. She was surprised though that Col. Fitzwilliam was so involved in searching for Lydia when his cousin could not run away fast enough. Perhaps having a member of the Army missing made Col. Fitzwilliam feel he had a duty.

"There is no use for us to stay awake," said Mr. Gardiner. "They will bring her here when they find her."

They climbed the stairs to their rooms, quiet except for the creaking of the steps.

Elizabeth brushed her hair and climbed into bed. The covers were already warm with a warming brick at her feet. "Poor Lydia." Her sister would be all alone and cold in the caves. Even though Mr. Wickham was a scoundrel, hopefully he had not deserted her. It would be terrifying to be lost in an underground cave in the dark. Elizabeth shivered.

She was so exhausted from worry that she quickly fell asleep to dreams of running in the dark, trying to find a way out from something. She would see Mr. Darcy yelling for help, but then he would turn his back on her and walk away.

Elizabeth woke to the sound of pounding in the hallway and loud voices. She jumped out of bed and pulled on a robe. Could Lydia have been found?

The room Elizabeth was in was really a servant's room. It was small and connected to the larger room the Gardiner's were in by a door. She did not have to go out in the hall but just through that door. She knocked, and her aunt opened it as if she had been standing there already.

"Has she been—"

"She has been found!"

Elizabeth and Mrs. Gardiner hugged fiercely.

"Come in. She has just arrived."

Elizabeth followed Mr. Gardiner through the connecting door to see Lydia bundled in blankets, pale and shivering.

Mr. Gardiner opened the room's door to admit servants carrying a tub. The inn's owner and wife carried in buckets of heated water.

"It was smart of you to order a hot bath to warm her up," Mrs. Gardiner complimented her husband.

Elizabeth noted that Mr. Gardiner seemed just as surprised to see the tub delivered. It was probably the owner's wife who thought of it. Elizabeth realized that there was a cost associated to the search for Lydia. A heated bath in the middle of the night could not be cheap.

Just then a platter of food arrived. She rubbed her forehead, as she knew Mr. Bennet could never repay the expenses her uncle had incurred on this trip.

Mrs. Gardiner led Lydia behind a screen to undress to get into the hot tub. Lydia had not even spoken, as she could not stop her teeth from chattering.

"When Lydia is warmed, we need to bring her down to the sitting room. They have not been able to question her."

Elizabeth turned to her uncle. "Question her as to why they did something so stupid? Could that not wait until the morning?"

Mr. Gardiner rubbed his face. "No, Mr. Wickham has not been found."

Elizabeth opened her mouth to ask for details, but her uncle held up his hand, and she closed her mouth.

"Everything I know is from what I was told by Col. Fitzwilliam. One of the search teams found her alone, huddled on the floor of a recessed cavern in one of the many tunnels. She shook her head when they asked if Mr. Wickham had harmed her."

Elizabeth closed her eyes and breathed out in relief.

"We are very fortunate."

Elizabeth's pain in her stomach came back when she realized that did not rule out her being compromised by Mr. Wickham willingly. She rubbed her forehead and wrapped an arm around her waist. Now they had to wait for Lydia to get warm and tell them what had happened.

11

Mr. Darcy settled accounts with the owner of the New Ship Inn regarding the extra food and the hot bath delivered to the Gardiner's room. Then he climbed back in his carriage for the quick trip to his inn for the last time that night. He would settle accounts with the owner in the morning. He dragged himself up the stairs and fell immediately into an exhausted sleep.

His valet woke him the next morning far too early for his being up half the night before. Then he saw his cousin asleep and drooling on the daybed. "What time did my cousin arrive last night?"

"I do not know. He came in so silently that I did not even hear him." His valet was a notoriously light sleeper. If Col. Fitzwilliam had not woken him, he must have been as silent as the fog.

Mr. Darcy was dying of curiosity to know what Lydia said about their mischief and if Wickham had been caught. But he let his cousin sleep. He silently washed, did his morning ablutions, and got ready for the day with his valet's help.

It was not until he was in the middle of his breakfast, the coffee was still hot, that he heard a groan from the direction of the other bed.

"Is that coffee?"

Mr. Darcy wiped his mouth with his serviette and chuckled. "You sound like a badger."

Col. Fitzwilliam stumbled out of the bed and fell into a chair at the table. The valet poured him a cup of coffee which his cousin drank swiftly, though it had been quite hot.

"Is that not burning your throat?"

"You learn to drink your coffee fast when you get it."

The more he learned about what Col. Fitzwilliam had to endure in the army, the more astonished he was that his cousin stayed in it. But then again, there were not many alternatives for a source of income for a second son of an Earl.

"Now that you are relatively awake and coherent,

tell me what you learned last night. First, what did Miss Lydia say, and was Wickham found?"

Col. Fitzwilliam leveled a flat stared his cousin. "I am going to need a lot more than coffee if you want me to talk at length." He tilted his head to the sumptuous breakfast laid out on the table. "I will eat while I talk."

Mr. Darcy nodded to his valet to order more food and then pushed the serving plates over within his cousin's reach.

After a few minutes of Col. Fitzwilliam inhaling a surprising amount of food, he began to talk. "Miss Lydia was found alone far from the pleasure gardens. She had initially run after Wickham, as he ran off nearly immediately."

He swallowed the rest of his coffee and motioned for a refill. "She tried to keep up with him, but she thought he had either been running or walking rapidly, as she lost him quite soon after running after him."

Col. Fitzwilliam bit off part of a scone and chewed. "They did have candles, but with the air in the caves and her running, the candle went out, and she was left alone in the dark. She yelled for any of them but heard nothing back."

He ate the rest of the scone and swallowed it

down with more coffee. "There was not just one cave, but many, with many tunnels branching off. Miss Lydia thought she had walked back the way they had come, but did not hear anything or see any light."

Col. Fitzwilliam swallowed the rest of his coffee. Mr. Darcy's valet immediately refilled it. "She came upon a small cave off the tunnel, and that was where she stayed. It was smart of her to stay put. She was easier to find that way, and she was quite far down into the tunnels. Miss Lydia was not sure if she had actually turned to go back to the well or if she had instead walked further away."

Mr. Darcy let his cousin finish the rest of the platters of breakfast food. Finally, Col. Fitzwilliam sat back in his chair with a sigh.

"What had their plan been?"

His cousin burst out with a short but a loud laugh. "What plan? There was no plan at all as far as Mrs. Forster and Miss Lydia were concerned. I imagine that Wickham's intent was on desertion."

It was as he had suspected. Mr. Darcy leaned back in his chair. Well, at least Elizabeth's sister was not hurt.

"Was Miss Lydia... ravished or compromised in any way?"

His cousin glanced at him sideways. "Different from being compromised by being lost in the caves with a man? No, it sounds like Wickham ran off immediately. She was lucky."

Mr. Darcy nodded. She was quite lucky from the stories he had been told about Wickham. But they were not only stories. All his by-blows were old enough now to be working at Pemberley. Even though he detested Wickham, he was not going to make his children suffer, nor the women he had abandoned.

"What happens now with Mr. Denny and Mrs. Forster? I cannot imagine her husband is very fond of her at this moment."

Col. Fitzwilliam shook his head and raised his eyebrows. "I have no idea." He took a healthy drink of his coffee before setting the cup back down again. "If she were my wife, she would be grounded forever. As a matter of fact, I would send her back to her relatives."

What would the Bennets do about their youngest? He was quite sure they would not allow her back at the camp. Mr. Gardiner seemed to have a good head on his shoulders, much unlike Mr. Bennet. Mr. Darcy was quite sure Mr. Gardiner would not let Lydia run wild nor allow this 'lark' to go unpunished.

As to how that would affect Elizabeth though, he did not know. He hoped it did not affect his chances at calling upon Elizabeth again. He had heard there were Roman ruins not too far from Brighton and thought a picnic lunch while exploring the ruins was an excellent idea.

ELIZABETH STARED out of the carriage window until a deep rut on the road threw her to the side so far that she had to turn her head to keep her balance. She stared at her younger sister on the other side of the carriage. Lydia had started out the trip sitting right next to her, but her whining and complaining had never ended, and so Mrs. Gardiner had switched seats with Lydia. Now Lydia sat on the opposite bench, sullen and pouting next to her uncle. But at least she was quiet.

Elizabeth was thrown against her aunt again by the rough road. The road from Brighton to the North Road was smooth and delightful travel. The Prince Regent had improved the roads for his friends from town to come to Brighton. But the roads in the rest of

England, especially it seemed the road that led to Meryton, was hard travel.

She turned her head to pretend she was looking out the carriage window as she wiped tears from her eyes. This was not due to the rough travel and bouncing of the carriage, even though she could imagine how sore she would be by the time they reached Longbourn. No, the tears were due to their leaving as early as possible that morning.

Mr. Gardiner would not even hear of Lydia going back to camp or even staying in Brighton so that she could continue to see her friends and attend the balls as Mrs. Forster's special companion. Elizabeth could not count the number of times Lydia said she was a 'special companion.'

As far as Mr. Gardiner was concerned, he was quite sure Lydia was no one's special companion anymore. He would not be surprised if Mrs. Forster herself were grounded by her husband.

That led to Lydia's screeching and stomping her feet. The Gardiners had never put up with that from their children, and they certainly were not going to put up with it from their niece who had cost them, the Army, and the townspeople of Brighton so much lost sleep, aggravation, and expense for the searches yesterday and last night. All of which Lydia seemed to think was her due and nothing out of the ordinary.

A quick pitcher of cold water on Lydia's face had her quieted down in a hurry. When she started her complaining up again, the pitcher of water from Elizabeth's room was used. If Lydia thought she could get away with tantrums in the carriage, she would be sorely mistaken, as Mr. Gardiner vowed he would make her get out and walk next to the carriage. By that time, Lydia had firmly believed they would do what they said and had not thrown another tantrum. If only her mother and father had employed such methods, then Lydia would have never grown up into this termagant.

Elizabeth sighed. All her ruminating about Lydia was just a tactic to distract herself from what was causing her chest to hurt. She would never see Mr. Darcy again.

Elizabeth had had a very small hope that she would see him before they left Brighton. That he might come to the inn, say his farewells, and ask Mr. Gardiner if he could call upon her in Meryton.

But no, they rose too early and left too quickly. She could also not forget how Mr. Darcy immediately took his leave from her at the pleasure gardens, as if he could not wait to leave.

She wiped her eyes again. It was stupid of her to ever think that Mr. Darcy would have renewed his proposal to her. After she had abused him to his face during her rejection of his proposal, and not only that, but abused him about matters that she did not even have correct. She groaned and put her head in her hand.

"Oh Lizzy," said Mrs. Gardiner rubbing Elizabeth's shoulder. "I know this road is hard. We shall soon be stopped to rest the horses and have tea."

Elizabeth nodded as she did not even want to try to speak. She would probably start sobbing instead, and then the whole story about Mr. Darcy would come out. They would not believe her one whit. Who would? She had never told them that Mr. Darcy had proposed to her when she was visiting Charlotte in Hunsford. Even if they had known that, the Gardiners would not have expected him to renew his addresses to her. Not after such a horrible set down during the rejection of his proposal. Especially when she had been wrong, oh so wrong about Wickham.

She shook her head. She had vowed since to never hear one side of the story and assume it was correct. Elizabeth had learned the hard way that people could act absolutely perfectly but yet be the worst lying scoundrels. At least her improvement was some good that had come out of that horrible day in Hunsford.

It was not only herself that had improved. Mr. Darcy had been absolutely wonderful. Such a gentleman to herself and her relatives. He had even called upon her that one day at the inn. They had gotten along so well in the pleasure gardens. Mr. Darcy had even moved closer to walk next to her. She was just so sure, and yet...

Elizabeth raised her head and looked out the carriage window again. It was no use thinking of what might have been. It was just a complete waste of her time. It was over, done with, that was it. Her focus now would be on weathering the scandal with her family. She hoped news had not reached Hertfordshire, but with Mrs. Forster, many townspeople, and soldiers involved in the search, she thought that hope was unrealistic.

At least Lydia had been found alone, but she had been lost for quite some time. There was no proof as to when exactly Wickham had left her. Elizabeth sighed. She hoped Lydia had told them the truth and that they would not see her increasing in just a few months. Because that would truly ruin the entire family's reputation.

12

"I see. Good day." Mr. Darcy turned away from the owner of New Ship Inn where Elizabeth and the Gardiners had been staying. They had departed quite early that morning, presumably to go back to Hertfordshire.

Mr. Darcy's lips turned down as he exited the inn and stepped up into his carriage. He sat on the bench seat and stared out the window. He could see the water, the waves breaking along the beach, couples walking and others braving the sea bathing machines. Everywhere he looked were people enjoying themselves, except for himself.

"Now what the blazes shall I do?" He had antici-pated seeing Elizabeth again. The Gardiners must have decided to leave posthaste, hoping to avoid the scandal. Or to arrive at Meryton before the scandal.

Mr. Darcy pounded on the roof of the carriage and told the driver to take him to the camp. Hopefully, he could catch his cousin before he left to meet him at the New Ship Inn. Col. Fitzwilliam was supposed to arrive there, where they would all depart for the Roman ruins together.

Mr. Darcy snorted. "Fat chance for that."

Damn, he was in a miserable mood now. On the short ride back to camp, Mr. Darcy considered leaving Brighton and following Elizabeth. He could then renew his courting of her and make sure she would give him a favorable answer before he talked to her father.

He leaned his head back on the side of the carriage and closed his eyes. He was still tired from spending much of the night working on the search effort for Elizabeth's youngest sister. Mr. Darcy was not sure Lydia's situation was a scandal. She had been found alone. Wickham, however, had not, and that was by far the biggest news in Brighton at the moment.

Perhaps the Gardiners had been worried that Lydia would have caused another scandal had she stayed in Brighton. Mr. Darcy snorted. He would not put it past that hoyden. He shook his head. He knew why she acted the way she did, and it was because the Bennets had absolutely no sense of parental duty. Again, it said much for the characters of the eldest two that they turned out so differently.

Now that the carriage had arrived at the military camp, Mr. Darcy climbed out.

His cousin approached. "Back so soon, Fitz?"

Mr. Darcy waited for him to walk closer so he would not have to shout. "They left early this morning right after the sun rose, according to the owner of the inn."

Col. Fitzwilliam whistled with raised eyebrows. "Well, that puts a fine point on that."

Mr. Darcy scowled and climbed back in his carriage, followed by his cousin.

"You should not be surprised, though. The Gardiners are good upstanding people, and Mr. Gardiner is certainly a gentleman even though he is in trade. They would want no hint of the scandal to affect Elizabeth or the rest of the Bennets. Or even their own children, assuming they have some?"

Mr. Darcy nodded. "Yes, their children are currently staying with the Bennets in Meryton."

"Well Fitz, what do you want to see today?"

Mr. Darcy gazed at his cousin who showed no ill

effects from being awake and working the majority of the night. All Mr. Darcy wanted was to either follow Elizabeth to Meryton or pull up and go back to Pemberley. He was now soured on Brighton completely.

"Do not tell me that you are moping over the loss of one Miss Bennet?"

Mr. Darcy scowled.

Col. Fitzwilliam laughed. "Well, I see. You are more smitten by her than I had thought. Go to her. Perhaps you could marry her before the scandal hits. It is too bad you will have the youngest sister as your sister-in-law, though. I would keep her away from Georgiana. We would not want any bad manners to rub off on her."

Mr. Darcy had not been in the mood to hear the truth about his beloved's family. "I have a mind to throw you out of the carriage."

Col. Fitzwilliam smiled. "I would like to see you try."

When Mr. Darcy did not speak Col. Fitzwilliam shook his head. "I say there are only two ways for you to get over this, Fitz. Either lose yourself in your cups or find another women to be agog over."

Mr. Darcy shook his head. "You never told me what Col. Forster said about the whole matter."

Col. Fitzwilliam snorted. "He was quite angry at the soldiers for taking his wife and her friend down into the caves but also at Wickham getting lost or deserting. Denny has been punished and has potato peeling duty for a month. Mrs. Forster has been forbidden to leave camp for how long I know not. Early this morning, Col. Forster dispatched a letter to the Gardiners that Miss Lydia was not welcome back at camp."

Mr. Darcy's eyebrows rose. "I see. He is not brushing this off on the Bennets, is he?"

"Not at all. It is about time he took his wife to hand. She and Miss Lydia had been flirting with all the officers ever since they had arrived." Col. Fitzwilliam shook his head.

"I wonder if that letter reached the Gardiners and prompted their leaving Brighton?" Mr. Darcy shrugged. "We will never know, will we?"

Mrs. Bennet was at first surprised, then squinting at the approach of the Gardiner's carriage at Longbourn. When she heard the reason why they had come back early, the screeching gave Elizabeth a headache. She climbed the stairs to lay down on her bed. But that was not far enough away to not hear her mother.

"What horrible treatment they have given my dear Lydia. To throw her out of camp! And after telling her she was a special companion, too."

Elizabeth rolled her eyes heavenward, took off her slippers, and crawled into bed under the blankets. She was so exhausted from that horrible trip home. With Lydia pouting and sullen, being jostled nearly half the ride back, Elizabeth was dead tired and sore.

Footsteps approached the bedroom door, the door creaked open and closed, there were more footsteps, and then the bed sunk on the other side. Elizabeth groaned.

"Oh Lizzy, you are being as dramatic as Mama."

Elizabeth pulled the covers off her head and frowned at Jane. "If you had been in that carriage on the way home, you would have the exact same sentiments."

Jane smiled and laid down next to Elizabeth on top the covers. "What did happen in Brighton?"

Elizabeth groaned and pulled the covers up to cover her head, but Jane's hand held them back.

Elizabeth put her forehead down on the pillow. "I do not even know where to start."

She turned her head to face Jane and then told her of the wonderful time they had had, and then she told of Lydia's behavior at the assembly, at the pleasure gardens, in the line to get ices, and finally her idea of going down in the caves and then getting lost.

By the end of Elizabeth's tale, Jane had covered her mouth, and her eyes could not possibly get any bigger. "Oh my. And Col. Forster really sent a letter stating that Lydia could not go back to the camp?"

Elizabeth nodded. "That was the most humiliating part. Well, besides how embarrassingly Lydia behaved in front of Mr. Darcy and his cousin. That letter was absolutely mortifying."

Jane rubbed Elizabeth's back and made calming noises. "I know you must think this is horrible, but Lydia was not compromised," at this, Elizabeth scoffed, "and you are all back here hale and hearty."

"Jane, I cannot understand why you think that our family is not ruined. Lydia went down in the caves and was lost with a man who was not her relative. The fact that they found her alone is good. Perhaps we can hide this until the soldiers send letters home to their family and describe the scandal that Lydia caused."

Jane leaned back against the headboard with a frown. "No, I do not see how she is compromised. She was not found with Wickham. They did behave foolishly by going down in the caves, but they started out with two men and two women. That is a perfectly respectable grouping."

Elizabeth rolled on her side, the better to make her argument. "We do not know when Wickham abandoned Lydia. She *says*," she spoke louder to stop Jane from speaking as she had opened her mouth, "that Wickham ran off immediately. But perhaps they both ran off to a secluded cave, and in a few months time we will see Lydia increasing."

Jane's mouth was agape. "You cannot certainly think that of our own sister, Elizabeth."

"I most certainly can. You were not there to see Lydia carrying on and flirting with officers most outrageously at the camp and wherever she went. She was the most unmitigated flirt!"

"But that does not mean that she would have... well.... Lydia would know what damage that would cause, not only to her reputation, but to her entire family. Plus, she would have to be sent away. She knows all that. I do not think she did that with Wickham."

"Well, I guess we will see in a few months time who was right."

Jane narrowed her eyes as she studied her sister. "What else is bothering you, Lizzy? Normally you are short only when you are upset about something."

Elizabeth closed her eyes. "I am sorry, Jane. I did not mean to be so short with you. But you are correct, and I do not want to talk about it."

Jane leaned forward. "You will feel better after you share your problem with me. You always do. Perhaps it is not so bad?"

Elizabeth scoffed. "Oh, it is very bad indeed. Fine, I shall tell you. Prepare yourself for tears."

Elizabeth then told her sister about Mr. Darcy in Brighton. All her thoughts, her astonishment at his improved behavior, growing close to him, and then his abrupt departure when Lydia was first lost in the caves.

"Well?" asked Elizabeth. "Even you cannot find any good in that story."

Jane leaned back against the headboard with her arms crossed and chewed on her bottom lip. "Perhaps Mr. Darcy had left the pleasure gardens for another reason. Maybe he had gotten a letter from home and he needed to leave right away?"

Elizabeth scoffed. "Now Jane, you cannot find anything good about this. It was the scandal that drove him away, and I will never see him again."

Jane glanced down at her sister, who was looking

down at the bed and fingering a pattern in the bed cover. "I did not know that you had any fondness for him before you left for Brighton."

"I felt regret at what I had said to him in Hunsford, but no, I did not have any fondness. Not until I saw him with such changed behavior." She looked up at Jane. "He was such a gentleman, and his countenance when he smiled... oh, Jane." Tears ran down Elizabeth's face. She rolled over to hide her face in the blankets as Jane rubbed her shoulder, murmuring pleasantries.

13

"Well Fitz," said Col. Fitzwilliam, "I thought you would have stayed longer. At least a month."

Mr. Darcy pulled his gloves on. "I have business I need to take care of back at Pemberley."

His cousin lifted an eyebrow and gave Mr. Darcy a flat stare. "If you are going to lie to me, you are going to have to do better than that."

Mr. Darcy looked up at his cousin with a frown. "I did not lie. I do have urgent business."

"Exactly what urgent business? You just came from there. There were no letters for you that arrived here."

Mr. Darcy lifted his head as he stared. "You sound like Aunt Catherine."

Col. Fitzwilliam raised his eyebrows. "You insult me?"

Mr. Darcy smirked. "You were the one questioning me about absolutely everything."

His cousin narrowed his eyes. "That was because you told one hell of a whopper and are denying it."

Mr. Darcy pulled off his gloves. He stared at them and then looked back up at his cousin. "Fine. I will tell you what my urgent business is. I warn you, I do not come out of this looking good. I look very bad indeed."

Col. Fitzwilliam did not say a word and crossed his arms.

Mr. Darcy smacked his right leg with his gloves. Then he told his cousin the sad tale of separating his close friend Mr. Bingley from Elizabeth's eldest sister. It was not until Elizabeth had rejected his offer of marriage and let him know in no uncertain terms how wrong he had been for destroying the happiness of her dear sister that he found out he and Mr. Bingley's sisters might have been in the wrong. Apparently, Jane had been greatly in love with Mr. Bingley.

Col. Fitzwilliam's lips were flattened, and he wore a frown upon his countenance. "That is very bad, Fitz. When you told me that tale at Rosings, I did not realize that was Elizabeth's eldest sister." He slowly shook his head. "You are going to have to fix this."

Mr. Darcy nodded. "I know. That is the urgent business that I need to take care of. I cannot myself go back to Meryton and court Elizabeth when I prevented Mr. Bingley from finding happiness with Elizabeth's eldest sister."

Col. Fitzwilliam nodded and smacked his cousin on the arm. "I completely understand. I hope he does not thrash you too much."

Mr. Darcy raised one eyebrow. "Have you seen me fence and box?"

Col. Fitzwilliam laughed. "Let me know if you need me to be your second."

Mr. Darcy shook his head. "I highly doubt Charles will call me out. It is more than likely he will forgive me immediately and rush back down to Meryton."

"If that were me, I would thrash you within an inch of your life. It is a good thing you have not done that to me."

Mr. Darcy narrowed eyes. "You do not fall in love every month wherever you go. Plus, you have never mentioned a woman. Ever."

Col. Fitzwilliam wiped the smirk off his face and looked much too bland. As if he were trying...

"You already have a woman!"

Col. Fitzwilliam stepped back and scoffed. "Me? When would I have time to court a woman? I am always going hither and thither for the Army. The Army is a cruel mistress."

Mr. Darcy smirked. "If you did not have a woman, you would have made some sort of joke, not tried to look innocent. That is how I know that you have one."

Col. Fitzwilliam laughed, but it sounded quite forced to Mr. Darcy's ear.

"Fine, you keep your secrets, Richard. One of these days, I will find out."

Col. Fitzwilliam shook his head and told his cousin to leave already. They said their farewells then Darcy pounded on the roof of the carriage to start the journey to London and Mr. Bingley. It was where they planned to go after Mr. Darcy departed Pemberley for Brighton.

Col. Fitzwilliam stood with his arms crossed and watched his cousin's carriage roll out of the camp. When he made sure that Mr. Darcy's carriage could not be seen anymore, he quickly unbuttoned the top of his coat and reached inside to the hidden pocket he had sewn, right above his heart. He pulled out a well-worn piece of paper and stared at the likeness of a woman painted upon it.

IT HAD BEEN a fortnight since they had come back from Brighton. Mr. and Mrs. Gardiner had stayed but one day and then departed to go back to town with the children. Since then, they had often been subjected to Mrs. Bennet's diatribes about how cruel Mrs. Forster was for having used Lydia, and how mean Col. Forster was for banishing Lydia from the camp when she had done nothing wrong at all.

Lydia sulked, pouted, whined, and continued to play up how horrible she had been treated. That resulted in her getting many trinkets, baubles, and hats from Meryton. No matter how much Mrs. Bennet and Lydia asked, Mr. Bennet would not move on the idea of going to Brighton as a family.

"No, my mind is much the same." Mr. Bennet turned a page of *The Globe* he was holding. "You told me what a great adventure and good matchmaking opportunities this would be for Lydia, and look how it turned out. No, I am quite done with that town. I do not wish to see it, and we will not go."

Elizabeth and Jane both spent more time than usual out-of-doors, Elizabeth with her great walks and Jane with the picking of flowers and herbs and hanging them to dry. It was for those reasons that they missed seeing their aunt Mrs. Phillips walk up to Longbourn in great haste.

When Elizabeth walked in the house and untied her bonnet, she paused in the act of removing it from her head. There was an uproar, but she could not completely make out what Mrs. Bennet was screeching. Thinking of the sly admonishments her mother had sent her way the past fortnight over Elizabeth's inability to have kept Lydia from going down the cave and not preventing Lydia getting kicked out of camp, Elizabeth avoided the sitting room and instead climbed up the stairs to her bedroom.

It was not until after she had changed out of her walking dress and into a day dress that was not covered with dust that Jane burst in. "Lizzy, you will not believe the news."

Elizabeth turned quickly. "You may tell me the news while you button me up."

Jane rushed over rolling her lips and shaking her head.

"What is it? It must be something with the way you are acting."

"I do not know what to think. Our aunt Mrs. Phillips was here, and she brought news that... that Mr. Bingley has come back to Netherfield."

Elizabeth stood stock still. "She is sure?" It would be horrible indeed if Mrs. Phillips had gotten the information wrong. It would be cruel to Jane.

"There, it is all buttoned."

Elizabeth quickly turned around and held Jane's hands which were trembling. "How are you?"

Jane gave her a little smile and shook her head. "I do not know what to think. I vow to not have it affect me." Jane held her head up with that declaration.

Elizabeth rolled her lips to prevent herself from smiling at the fact that Jane's hands were still trembling in hers. "That is a good plan."

"I will treat him just as if he is an acquaintance that I once knew. Nothing else. Nothing special."

Elizabeth nodded her head. "That is exactly what I would to. No need to spend any extra time talking to him or doing anything other than just basic greetings."

Elizabeth squeezed her sister's hands and thought of Mr. Bingley's friend. Would he have accompanied Mr. Bingley down to Netherfield again? She swallowed. No, he would have no reason to, especially if he wanted to avoid Lydia and the Bennets due to the Brighton scandal.

Elizabeth smiled brightly at her sister and ignored the pain in her chest. She knew that if she smiled really widely, she would not cry.

14

M r. Darcy pulled on his gloves, accepted his beaver hat and riding crop.

"Hurry up, old man!"

Mr. Darcy raised his eyes and leveled a flat stare upon his friend.

"Oh no, Fitzwilliam. You owe me after what you did. You are not getting out of going to Longbourn with me." Mr. Bingley bounced on the balls of his feet and did not stop beaming.

Mr. Bingley had been like this ever since he had gotten over his shock and anger at what his close friend and both of his sisters had done. Mr. Bingley would make them all eat crow.

Mr. Darcy settled his hat upon his head and turned away without a word to walk to their horses.

"Is this is not a fine day? It is absolutely beautiful in Hertfordshire. I have always said so. I do so like the country. It is so refreshing, and the air is simply clean and... well, I guess I shall just have to say refreshing again."

Mr. Darcy rolled his eyes heavenwards.

Thankfully, during their ride to Longbourn, he did not have to hear anymore cheerful words out of his friend's mouth. Mr. Bingley had dismounted and knocked at the door before Mr. Darcy had even brushed the dust off himself. A servant took care of the horses, and they were led into the sitting room, which was populated by every one of the Bennet daughters and Mrs. Bennet.

The pleasantries were observed, and then the two men sat in chairs that faced Mrs. Bennet, as they were the only chairs available.

Mrs. Bennet acted predictably according to Mr. Darcy. She fawned over Mr. Bingley and ignored him completely. He spent time glancing around the room because he could not see Elizabeth from his vantage point. To do so, he would have to lean forward. Since he could not, due to manners, he looked at everything but Mrs. Bennet.

When Mrs. Bennet admonished Mr. Bingley for leaving Netherfield when he had promised to dine at Longbourn, Mr. Darcy stood abruptly and walked to the back of the room to stand in front of a window. He held his hands behind his back and pursed his lips.

He had nearly forgotten how absolutely horrid Elizabeth's mother was. There was nothing outside to focus on, but then he noticed the reflection in the window. It was of the table, and more specifically, Elizabeth. He stood and watched her stare at his back for some time before she looked back down to her needlework. But she did not actually pull her needle and thread for quite some time.

Did that mean that she had feelings for him? He had not been sure what reception he would receive from her. He did not think that she had been polite in Brighton to pass the time, as that would not have been like her. Mr. Darcy swallowed and hoped that she did indeed have feelings for him, but he had to make sure. Unfortunately, the only way to be sure would be to ask her, and he would never do that again unless he knew absolutely and unequivocally that the answer to his question would be a resounding yes.

Mr. Darcy turned back to the room when Mrs.

Bennet invited Mr. Bingley, and Mr. Bingley only, to supper the day next. Mr. Darcy glanced at Elizabeth to see that she had closed her eyes, and a slow blush was appearing on her neck and cheeks.

He should cut this visit short before Mrs. Bennet mortified her daughter any further. Mr. Darcy walked to stand in front of Mrs. Bennet. "I must take my leave."

A creak of furniture and bootsteps meant that Mr. Bingley stood by him as well. Good. He could not stand one more minute of Mrs. Bennet.

They made their farewells and left to mount their horses and ride back to Netherfield. Mr. Darcy set the brisk pace, as he did not want to hear his friend's effusive praise. He was sure to get enough of that back at Netherfield, and his feelings were too raw for him to deal with his friend in love.

Mr. Darcy was first back at Netherfield. He jogged up the stairs and almost threw his riding accouterments at his valet. He then stormed down the hall, mumbling to himself with such a scowl on his countenance that Miss Bingley, instead of giving him a cheerful greeting, turned to the side and backed away. Mr. Darcy had ample room to walk past her down the hall to the game room, where he picked up a billiard ball and rolled it down the billiard table until it slammed into the side.

"Get ahold of yourself," said Mr. Darcy. "What are you, a coward or a man? You did not work so hard to improve yourself to go back to that same prideful peacock that you were before! Get a grip, Fitzwilliam." That last line was punctuated by yet another billiard ball slamming into the back wall of the billiard table.

"Fitzwilliam!" Mr. Bingley stood just inside the game room, aghast at his friend."What in the devil are you doing? You completely scared my sister, Caroline!"

Mr. Darcy turned around and saw that, indeed, Miss Bingley and Mrs. Hurst were peering into the doorway of the game room. He closed his eyes and took several deep breaths. Then he opened them. "I apologize. Please forgive me."

The women muttered some pleasantries but did not leave the doorway.

Mr. Bingley stepped closer to his friend until he could speak without his sisters hearing. "What is wrong? We just came from Longbourn. Nothing could have happened on the way back to make you this upset."

Mr. Darcy clenched his fists and looked at his

friend. "No, nothing happened on the way back. It is what happened at the Bennets. I am most furious with how I behaved."

His friend blinked with his mouth agape. "You acted perfectly well, Fitzwilliam. You were the model of propriety." He spoke quite slowly, as if to a deranged man.

Mr. Darcy fiercely shook his head. "No, you do not understand. I have worked hard to improve myself, to never be as I was before so proud and conceited, yet there I just was, and I said not even a word. What must she think of me?"

Mr. Bingley stared at his friend. "Mrs. Bennet?"

The combined look of fear and distaste on his friend's countenance drew Mr. Darcy out of his anger and brought a smile to his face.

"Oh Charles, do think I have more sense than that. No, Miss Elizabeth."

Mr. Bingley's eyebrows rose so high they were lost in the blond curls hanging down over his forehead.

"Oh come now," said Mr. Darcy. "Did you not know I was fond of her?"

Mr. Bingley opened his mouth, closed it, then shook his head.

Mr. Darcy scowled. Then he turned away and

stomped to the end of the game room. He fiddled with billiard sticks in their holder. If his friend, who he was with every day, had not even known he was fond of Elizabeth, then it was no surprise at all that she had no idea when he had proposed to her in Hunsford. Damn and blast.

He slammed a billiard stick down into the holder and turned around to ask his friend a question but stopped when he saw that Mr. Bingley's sisters were still huddled in the doorway. He closed his mouth. He did not want them to know who he had a tendre for, unless he wanted to be teased about it *ad nauseam.*

Instead, he walked back to Mr. Bingley and asked if he wanted to go back to Longbourn.

AFTER BOTH MEN HAD LEFT, Elizabeth set down her needlework, rushed into the hallway, gathered her bonnet and Spencer jacket, and rushed out of the house. She felt so stupid. How could she have thought that he had feelings for her? That they had formed some sort of connection? He had done nothing but stand and brood like he used to do.

"He barely even glanced in my direction. No, he

did not even once glance in my direction!" Elizabeth kicked a rock out of her way as she stomped on her well-worn path. Her fists were clenched, her eyes narrowed. "Of all the conceited, prideful jackanapes!"

She could not believe she had thought that he had changed. Worse, she could not believe that she had feelings for him. That she had cried over him.

"Ugh." She growled loud enough to frighten several birds out of the nearby trees. "And that is entirely the fault of Mr. Darcy, too."

Elizabeth continued to stomp and mutter her way to the top of Oakham Mount. There she took several deep calming breaths and admired the wondrous views of the countryside. A smile returned to her face, and she felt calm again.

Until it was broken by Kitty. "Elizabeth! Elizabeth! You must come! Mr. Darcy is here to call upon you!"

Elizabeth frowned and turned. "What? Did you say Mr. Darcy was here? To call upon me?"

She walked to the edge of the hill. Kitty was on the path below, panting. "Yes." Kitty leaned over resting her hands on her legs. "You must come. No one knows what to say to him."

Elizabeth rose an eyebrow. Oh. Well, she had plenty to say to him.

She strode back down the hill. So Mr. Darcy had come back, had he? She was curious to hear what he had to say for himself. It was not like she had any formal relationship with him, could not claim any sort of anything at all, but they had formed a friendship in Brighton. She swore he had had a tendre for her. She knew she had one for him. Whether she still did remained to be seen.

Elizabeth walked in the back of the house, took off her bonnet and jacket, and shoved it at Hill. She was not going to go change into another dress. If she had dust on this one, well, he would just have to deal with it.

She walked into the sitting room and saw her mother staring at Mr. Darcy, Mr. Darcy staring at her, Lydia absent, and Jane pleading with her eyes. Pleasantries were exchanged, and Elizabeth sat down at the table in the same position she had occupied before.

The silence was deafening. Elizabeth worked on her needlework but could not remember the pattern, so she stabbed at the fabric and pulled the needle through just to have something to do. She could hear the birds outside, the room was so quiet.

Finally, there was a creak of the furniture from the direction of Mr. Darcy and a cough. "How did you find your travel back from Brighton?"

Elizabeth paused in her stabbing the fabric. He opened with that?

Her head rose to stare at him. She studied him. He sat perfectly straight, hands on his thighs, and looked uncomfortable and ill at ease. Her peakedness turned to understanding. Mr. Darcy was nervous. "The road from Brighton to the North Road was quite nice. But after that, it were uncomfortable and not smooth."

Mr. Darcy gave a quick nod. He stared at her.

Elizabeth gave him a quick smile then looked back down at her needlework to find that she had pulled the thread through over and over in the exact same spot. She would have to undo that, but it would leave a big hole. Well, that was another piece ruined.

She peeked up at him to see that he still stared at her. Why had he even come?

"And your aunt and uncle, did they make it back to town safely?"

"Yes, they did. Thank you for asking." This had to be the most tedious, most drawn out conversation in the history of man.

Elizabeth glanced at her mother to see that she

just stared at Mr. Darcy. Thank goodness she was not saying anything.

"The day you departed Brighton, I had thought to ask you to tour the Roman ruins. They are just north of Brighton."

Elizabeth smiled and sat down her needlework. "Oh, that would have been delightful. I have never seen a Roman ruin. I would have loved to explore that, dearly."

Mr. Darcy's lips turned upward.

That would have been the most wonderful outing. She could imagine them talking for hours, admiring fallen columns. Oh Lydia, she had to go and ruin it all.

Running footsteps approached, then her youngest sister burst into the sitting room.

"Mama! I want to go to Meryton with Kitty. I am so bored here! There is nothing to do. I want to go back to Brighton." Lydia stood in front of her mother, then turned to gaze at the rest of the room. "Lord, what are you doing here?"

The eldest two sisters gasped, "Lydia!"

Elizabeth glanced at Mr. Darcy to find his countenance had reverted to aloof and withdrawn.

"Lydia, my dear," said Mrs. Bennet with a glance at Mr. Darcy, "you know that is not how I raised you."

Another glance at Mr. Darcy. "Show your proper manners."

Lydia scoffed then turned back to her mother. "But—"

"LYDIA."

Lydia spun around with her wide eyes and her chin jutted out. She then slowly curtsied quite low, which was perfect for a Duke, not a member of the upper class.

Elizabeth closed her eyes and rubbed her forehead.

15

Mr. Darcy stared at the wall to the side of Mrs. Bennet. His cousin's words were loud in his head. *It is too bad you will have the youngest sister as your sister-in-law, though. I would keep her away from Georgiana. We would not want any bad manners to rub off on her.*

Mrs. Bennet opened her mouth, but Mr. Darcy abruptly stood. "Excuse me, I must take my leave."

He quickly bowed and quit the room. He took the reins off of the hitching post, not waiting for a servant, mounted his horse, and kicked it into a canter. He left the grounds of Longbourn and rode over the meadows towards Netherfield.

As he approached, he turned his horse's head and instead rode through more of the Hertfordshire countryside. He could not go back to Netherfield just yet. There would be questions and smiles as to how the visit went. Miss Bingley would probably make accurate observations as to how the Bennet family had behaved. He could not to go back. Not until he got his thoughts in order.

He had a duty to the Darcy name, the Pemberley estate, and all those who looked upon the Darcy name for their living. He needed a wife of good character, good manners, and breeding. His younger sister was almost ready to have her season, and she needed good examples of proper comportment. All these thoughts circled in his head, along with his cousin's words.

His horse was breathing heavily, and he was sweating himself, so finally he turned his horse's head back towards Netherfield.

After handing off his hat, gloves and writing crop to his valet, Miss Bingley was one of the first to approach him in the hallway. With how quickly she appeared, she must have been waiting for him to come back to Netherfield.

"Good day, Mr. Darcy." Miss Bingley sidled closer. "I hear you called upon the Bennets with my brother?" She stood waiting with a mischievous smile on her countenance.

"I did. If you would excuse me." Mr. Darcy walked up the staircase to his room.

He ordered a bath and removed his now dusty and sweaty clothes. He sat in the bath and still had no idea as to what course of action he should take. Offer for Elizabeth again or find a wife from a respectable family with connections?

He groaned and leaned back in the tub. If his aunt ever found out he was seriously considering asking Elizabeth to marry him, again, she would have him immediately locked up in Bedlam. He flattened his lips. He could expect trouble from his aunt Lady Catherine de Bourgh no matter who he married because he certainly was not marrying her daughter, his cousin.

He had never found anyone who would bewitch and beguile him like Elizabeth Bennet. And that was the problem. Was he thinking of his duties as the caretaker of the Darcy name and the great Pemberley estate? Or was he thinking of himself? Did he really want to have *that woman*, Mrs. Bennet, for his mother-in-law and that hoyden for his sister-in-law?

ELIZABETH SAT down after Mr. Darcy abruptly left. It was as if her legs had ceased functioning and could not hold her up anymore. It happened so suddenly, she could not even get her thoughts together. One moment he was there, and then he was gone. It all happened after Lydia had entered the room, insulted and then mocked him with her curtsy.

She covered her mouth with her hand and rushed from the room. She nearly ran in her haste to get out of the house, away from Lydia, her mother and her father who did nothing about their behavior.

She did not stop to get her bonnet or jacket. She did not care if her skin turned brown or she got more freckles. It did not even matter.

Elizabeth ran along her path up the hill as far she could until she bent over panting. Then she walked the rest of the short way up to the top of Oakham Mount. Of course her eyes were immediately drawn to the chimneys and rooftop of Netherfield.

She collapsed on the ground and held her face in her hands. "He's never coming back again. Never. Never, never, never."

She finally let herself cry. Great, wrenching, sobbing cries as she rocked herself back and forth.

Her dress would get dirty, but she could not fathom an ounce of concern. Nothing seemed to matter anymore. Why should she care that she looked presentable? Why should she care that her dresses stayed perfect when the most perfect man who she thought she had lost in Brighton, who had come back to her, when reminded of her family's ill behavior, rushed out of the room as if his coat was on fire?

Elizabeth sat there and cried until she could not cry anymore. Then she wiped her face dry and stared around her numbly. She looked down and pulled at the grass. She did turn herself, though, so she was not facing Netherfield, and not Longbourn, either. She could not bear to see her home, the source of her misery right now.

Maybe that was what she needed. Elizabeth lifted her head up. She could leave Longbourn. The only thing keeping her here was her father and Jane. Well, that and she did not have anywhere else to go. But what if she did have somewhere else to go? She could move to town and live with the Gardiners while she devoted herself to finding a husband. Because she clearly was not going to find one around here.

The thought of Mr. Darcy at Netherfield courting another woman physically hurt. Elizabeth pressed a fist to her chest. But she would not think of him anymore. She had a new life to plan. She would miss Jane dearly, but they could write. She would tell her sister all about her attending balls, routs and assemblies to find a man she loved dearly.

There was no use in her staying here anymore. Jane would be marrying soon and living with... his good friend. Jane would have a life of her own and children soon. Yes, Elizabeth needed to go away to find her husband.

"I could help the Gardiner's children. I could be a governess for them and still look for a husband. It will work out completely. I must write them at once." She stood, brushed off her dress, and walked down the hill.

How soon could she leave for London? She would write to her aunt and uncle immediately. Then she would go through her things and leave what she did not need to bring with her.

She felt much better when she reached the bottom of the hill. A small part of her felt that she was acting without having all the information. She did not know if Mr. Darcy would ever see her again.

But she shook her head. If she were Mr. Darcy, she would have nothing to do with this family. Plus, she did not think that his feelings for her were strong enough to put up with her family. Not if he ran off when Lydia found herself in scandal or when her family behaved horribly.

No, Elizabeth was certain her only future lay in moving to London.

16

M r. Darcy avoided Longbourn while his thoughts were unsettled. Mr. Bingley rode over there by himself, which was no hardship for him. He had gotten himself engaged to Jane the day after Mr. Darcy's abrupt departure from Longbourn.

His friend could easily handle the ill behavior of Mrs. Bennet, the youngest three daughters, and Mr. Bennet. His friend had an easy-going manner and was delighted with everything. Plus, he did not need a wife with requirements for the legacy of an old name and wealthy estate. Mr. Bingley only needed to look for a gentlemen's daughter, and he had found one.

Mr. Darcy sighed. He longed for Elizabeth to be

at Pemberley with him. He could see her there with their children, smiling, laughing. His lips turned up just thinking about it. But he could not stand being around her mother or her younger sisters, who would probably push themselves into their lives unexpectedly and without prior notice. He could not subject his younger sister to them. He did not want anyone he knew, barely knew, or did not even know to find them at Pemberley. He no longer wore a smile.

He had struggled with this decision and could not decide upon a course of action. He knew what he wanted, but he also knew what his duty was.

This evening's supper would be a trial for him. Miss Bingley had invited Jane and a companion over for supper. Of course her companion would be Elizabeth. He had reminded himself to act normally but had delayed going downstairs so long that he was late.

He walked into the dining room without glancing at the other occupants. He would sit down before he looked at Elizabeth.

But he did not see her at all. Instead, he saw one of her younger sisters. The girl was subdued and quiet. He could not even remember her name.

Well, Elizabeth having not attended was a logical

move on her part, but it still brought a pang to his chest. He had looked forward to and yet dreaded seeing her again. Was she hurt by his abrupt departure the other day?

Now that he had arrived, the first course was served. He let the conversation flow around him, not even bothering to interject his thoughts.

"I am surprised to see that you did not bring Miss Elizabeth. Is she unwell?" Miss Bingley asked.

Mr. Darcy's head snapped up at the thought of Elizabeth unwell.

Her sister looked decidedly uncomfortable. "Elizabeth could not make it tonight. She is well, but she is leaving for London in the morning."

"She is visiting her aunt and uncle there?" He blurted his question without remembering that he had wanted to be aloof regarding her.

Jane looked at him with a frown. "No. She plans to stay in London with our aunt and uncle."

He stared. The news lanced through his chest like a physical blow. "She is leaving?" He repeated it like a dunderhead, but he could not fathom that Elizabeth was leaving.

"I would not mind staying in town," said Miss Bingley. Mrs. Hurst hummed her agreement. "There is much to do and see there, unlike the country."

Jane looked down at her lap, then quickly glanced at Mr. Bingley.

Mr. Darcy turned to his friend, who also looked decidedly uncomfortable and was also avoiding his eyes. What the deuces was going on? "What is the reason for her leaving for London? A holiday in town and then home again before the snows fall?"

"Who would not want to go to town to escape the countryside?" asked Miss Bingley.

Mr. Bingley still avoided his eyes and stared at his betrothed. Mr. Darcy looked back at Jane.

"One could entertain themselves for weeks," said Miss Bingley. "Even months in town without visiting the same entertainments twice."

Jane finally lifted her head and stared at Mr. Darcy with a frown and her lips turned down. "Elizabeth said there is no future for her here. She will only marry for love, but as that is not likely here, she is moving to town to find a better class of men and a love match."

"What?" Every single word she had said speared his heart.

Jane's words had done the deed of clearing up his thoughts, stripping away everything else to leave only that what mattered.

He stood abruptly, his chair sliding back on the Persian carpet with ease. "If you will excuse me."

He threw down his serviette and quit the room, walking quickly while he yelled for his valet.

The words of Elizabeth's sister floated in his head. *She had no future here. She thought no love match would ever be found here and therefore was moving to find a 'better class of men' and a 'love match'.* Mr. Darcy scoffed. A better class of man? No love match?

Damn him for being such a coward. Why had he ever listened to his cousin in the first place? He was not going to let Elizabeth marry a dandy from London. No one would treat her right. They would try to curtail her spirit, her liveliness, her reading books. No, he would not allow that to happen.

ELIZABETH FINISHED FOLDING HER NEEDLEWORK, such as it was, and pushed it down into her trunk. She wondered what was happening at Netherfield at that moment. Would Mr. Darcy even care that she was not there? Would he act like it was a supper on any other day? Elizabeth clenched her jaw and pushed that thought away. She forbade herself to think of him anymore.

She turned away from her trunk and looked around the room. On the morrow, she only had to pack her things that she used every day, such as her hairbrush, and she would be ready to leave.

Elizabeth twisted her lips. She would miss her walks in the countryside. But she knew she could not stay here when *he* was at Netherfield. She could not be reminded of him with Jane married to *his* good friend. She would come back for the wedding, of course, but she would leave immediately thereafter. It would be cruel to stay longer otherwise.

There was a knocking at the front door, which was unusual, as callers always came in the morning. She expected to hear her aunt Mrs. Phillips but instead heard the deep voice of Mr. Darcy.

A stab of pain lanced her chest. What was *he* doing here?

Elizabeth quickly walked over to her bedroom door and closed it. She did not want to hear his voice. She bit her lips. Had something happened to Jane?

She heard stomping up the staircase, footsteps rapidly approached her door, and then a knock. She opened the door to find Hill. "Excuse me, Miss Elizabeth, but Mr. Darcy wants to speak with you."

He was here for her. Her bruised heart tingled

with happiness, but she fiercely collected herself. She had already made up her mind, and nothing he had to say could change her opinion of the matter. "I am sorry, Hill. Please send him away."

Elizabeth closed the door and swallowed, hoping to stave off her tears. She did not want to marry a man who had run away from the hint of scandal and did not even help, unlike his cousin. Or ran at the first sign of impropriety, though she had to admit Lydia's behavior the other day was absolutely horrid.

That was another reason she was leaving Longbourn. She could not stand that her father continued to brush off her pleas and let Lydia and Kitty run wild. Nor could she stand her own mother's humiliating behavior.

No, she was not staying. Elizabeth had admitted that there was no Mr. Bingley in her future here. She would not wait around to be a spinster, to live on the charity of relatives as an old maid. Though she would love to read and play with Jane's kids, even though—

A loud voice filtered up from downstairs. Elizabeth stood still and listened but could not make out any words. Now she heard her mother's distinctive voice. She took at step to her door.

"What is going on down there?" Lydia cried.

Elizabeth bit her lip. What *was* going on downstairs?

Her door burst open with Lydia. "Lizzy, you must come down and see Mr. Darcy! Mama says you have to!"

Elizabeth frowned and pursed her lips. Now that her bedroom door was open, she could hear her mother assuring Mr. Darcy that Elizabeth would see him and not to worry. She scoffed.

She could not imagine why he had called upon her, and in the evening, too. If Jane had been in trouble, a servant would have been sent to Longbourn with a letter or message. Since Jane was not in trouble, why he was even here? What did he have to say to her?

There was no reason for her to go downstairs and listen to whatever he had to say. His running out of the room at Lydia's behavior, along with his silence for the last few days, was enough for her to know that he was not the man she wanted for a husband. The pain in her chest gave lie to that statement, but nothing would induce her to walk down those steps.

"Good evening, Mr. Darcy," said Mr. Bennet. "For what purpose do we owe the pleasure of your visit?

It must be something quite urgent for you to call in the evening?"

Elizabeth bit her lip.

"I wish to speak to Miss Elizabeth."

Mrs. Bennet interjected. "She will not come downstairs! I have sent Lydia to bring her down, but she will not come down and listen to Mr. Darcy!"

Elizabeth covered her face with her hands and leaned against the wall in her bedroom. This had to be the most mortifying experience of her life.

"If you will excuse me, Mr. Darcy, I will speak to my daughter."

Floorboards creaked, then heavy footsteps ascended the staircase and grew louder on the hallway floor. Elizabeth sighed and peeked through her fingers. Mr. Bennet stood at the doorway with his hands behind his back. "Now Lizzy, tell me, why will you not go downstairs to receive Mr. Darcy? He is the type of man to whom I would not refuse anything."

Elizabeth stood straight and lowered her hands. "Papa, he has nothing to say that I want to hear."

"I am quite surprised by his visit." He paused, but Elizabeth did not respond. "Well, you had better go downstairs and hear what he has to say. I can only think of one reason why a gentleman would call after hours urgently demanding to speak to a woman in the house."

She looked heavenwards. "I am not getting betrothed. I do not know why he is here, but it is certainly not for that."

Mr. Bennet studied his daughter. "I do not think you have even spoken to him much."

Elizabeth pursed her lips and fingered her dress material. "He was at Rosings Park when I went to visit Charlotte. So we dined several times a week with him."

"There must have been some discussion with him in Brighton, from what your uncle told me?"

Elizabeth closed her eyes and then opened them again. "Yes, there was." She tilted her head up. "But he left immediately when we realized Lydia was lost in the caves with Mr. Wickham. He did not even stay to help. Then, just a few days ago when Lydia behaved ill, again Mr. Darcy could not quit Long-bourn fast enough."

Mr. Bennet frowned. "That is upsetting, but can you blame him? I myself stay in my study for that very reason."

Elizabeth sighed and looked to her left. She did not want to speak of her concerns about her father's lack of parental duty, again. She just wanted to leave Longbourn.

"Go downstairs, child, and see what he has to say."

Elizabeth sighed. She pushed her shoulders back, tilted her head up, and walked out of her bedroom to stand on a lower step, as she could go no further with her family, Mr. Darcy and servants at the bottom of the stairs.

"Miss Elizabeth, I... I heard you are moving to London on the morrow. Please, let me speak to you?"

17

M r. Darcy let out his breath. She stepped down the staircase without even glancing at him, but he could not stop gazing at her. At the bottom of the staircase, she curtsied and led the way to the sitting room. Elizabeth sat on a chair and pointedly looked across the room at the wall.

He sat in the chair across from her. The door to the sitting room was pulled shut.

"Please, leave the door open," cried Elizabeth.

Mr. Darcy stared at the only woman in England who would beg for a door to be left open when she was alone in a room with a wealthy, unmarried man. The servant pushed the door back open. He would not be surprised at all if he heard Mrs. Bennet scuffling in the hall right outside the door, listening.

"Thank you for seeing me." He watched her nod, but she would still not look at him. He frowned.

"I... I saw your sisters at supper at Netherfield."

She made no response or any sign that she had heard him. This was going to be harder than he had thought. And more embarrassing, as her entire family could hear him. He had noticed that Mr. Bennet had not gone back to his study yet.

"Your eldest sister mentioned that you were leaving for London."

She nodded but did not respond.

He pursed his lips. This would not do. He was not going to have the most important discussion in his life with a statue. He stood abruptly, walked across the room to a window and turned around.

Elizabeth was in profile now. She still stared ahead with her back straight and her chin tilted up. He would have smiled at her obvious disdain for him if he had not been vexed as well.

"Could you at least do me the honor of facing me when I am speaking?"

She turned her head towards him, but that was all. This was ridiculous.

"Can you tell me what I have done for you to treat me in this manner?"

He glanced up at the movement by the door. Mrs. Bennet had peeked in quickly. He narrowed his eyes then looked back at the only woman that had ever driven him to vexation so easily.

"You want to know what you have done to anger me?" She sounded incredulous as if he had any idea of what she was distressed about.

Mr. Darcy flattened his lips and nodded. This entire conversation was not proceeding at all like he had expected. How had he lost control of it?

"On your last visit here, my youngest sister came into this room and displayed some ill behavior. I am not saying her behavior should be excused, but you departed immediately. And did not come back with Mr. Bingley."

Mr. Darcy liked Elizabeth when she was cheerful and smiling, but he had to admit that this vision of her with fire in her eyes was a close second.

"I am sorry." He clenched his jaw to stop from reminding her that he had mentioned her younger sister's behavior before.

Elizabeth's left eyebrow rose. "You have nothing more to say about why you left so quickly? Then what about your behavior when we realized that

Lydia was lost in the caves? You departed immediately as well."

Mr. Darcy put his hands behind his back. "I departed the pleasure gardens for the exact reason I stated at the time, which was that you were distressed, and I thought you would rather have me gone to not see you in distress."

He paused to study her, but she was unmoved by his explanation.

"I did go back to my inn, but it was to speak to the owner to order refreshments, hot beverages and blankets to be continually replenished throughout the night for the men searching for your sister." He paused to take several deep breaths as his voice had been quite loud.

"Your uncle helped me pick up and deliver those items all night until I brought him to your inn so that he could sleep and console both you and your aunt, as I knew neither of you would have been able to sleep."

He was gratified to finally see a change in Elizabeth's countenance. The fiery anger drained and left her pale. She swallowed and raised a hand to her mouth. All the while she stared at him.

The silence was such that he could hear the

crackling of the fire, the creaking of the floorboards in the hallway, and her mother's whispering.

He was vexed that again she had judged him and found him lacking. He wanted to be angry at her. But he realized that he had done the exact thing she had accused him of on that horrible day at the Hunsford Parsonage. He had been prejudiced against her family then and now. That was what had kept him away from her.

His vexation drained. Blazes and damnation. Had he again ruined any chance of a positive resolution to this conversation?

ELIZABETH COULD NOT BREATHE. She was gasping through her tight chest. How could she have done it again? She had been so angry, so sure he had fled in Brighton because of the scandal he did not want to be associated with, yet she had been so wrong. He had not fled it all but had helped all night.

She looked down and closed her eyes. A sob escaped. If only she could quit this room and run away, she would. Oh, how stupid was she? Leaving for London to find a love match with a gentleman that would not run from her family, and he had been here all along in Mr. Darcy.

Elizabeth hunched over in her chair. She could not bear to look at him. Her heart was breaking anew. She had been so stupid to hope he would renew his addresses to her, and she ruined it.

Now her future was set. She would go to London on the morrow and have to accept whatever came her way. No man would ever match the one she had lost. Another sob escaped. And another. Elizabeth covered her face with both hands. She was mortified that she was crying in front of him, but she did not seem to be able to stop herself.

"Miss Elizabeth, are you unwell? Do you need a glass of wine?"

She shook her head. He was such a gentleman. Another sob escaped at the thought of the woman that would be his wife. Some beautiful, caring, understanding, perfectly dressed at all times with no mud on *her* petticoats. Her headache pounded.

"Miss Elizabeth. Here, drink this. It will make you feel better."

She could not hide behind her hands waiting for him to leave. She could not be boorish to him again. Elizabeth lowered one hand and took the glass of wine, but her hand was trembling so badly that Mr. Darcy had to hold the glass and raise it to her lips.

She avoided looking at him still. She could not bear to see what he thought of her now. Why was he even still here? Could not someone ask him to leave?

Wood on wood scraping brought Elizabeth's head up to see Mr. Darcy dragging a chair next to hers. Her eyes widened, then she quickly lowered her head and stared at her dress. She saw his legs as he sat down next to her. She closed her eyes. Would this torment never end?

"Could you please tell me what has distressed you? I do not understand why my helping the search for your sister in Brighton caused you distress."

Elizabeth swallowed and picked at her dress. "I am relieved and happy and exceedingly grateful for all that you did for our family and for Lydia." She had to stop and compose herself again.

"You may thank me, but I thought only of yourself when I provided my help."

She quickly covered her face as tears welled up in her eyes. Could he not just leave her alone and get on with finding his perfect wife?

"Truly, please tell me what I have done or said to cause you this much distress? I am completely at a loss."

Elizabeth chuckled then wiped her tears. Maybe if he heard the truth, he would finally leave. She should count the seconds. It would be a record for him, she was sure. "You are the perfect gentleman. That is what you have done."

"I do not understand." Creaking from his chair.

Her head still bowed, she glanced to her left but still saw his seated legs. "Because I had foolishly thought... I was a nodcock and thought that you... had a tendre for me. But that is impossible now as I have just accused you of doing something you had not done." Just like in Hunsford. Her heart could not break anymore than it already had.

18

M r. Darcy sat back in his chair, poleaxed. He blinked and continued to stare at Elizabeth. He had no thoughts other than her words chasing around in his head. He was cautious; he did not want to make the same mistake he had previously, but he was quite certain she had implied... she had a tendre for him.

His heart sped up. He swallowed and sat up in his chair. A smile threatened to burst, but he was still not sure. He could not do this sitting down.

Mr. Darcy stood and pulled down the sleeves of his coat. No, he could not stand either because she was still staring down at her dress, but now with her hands covering her face again.

He walked away so that he could see her entirely,

but a loud, heart-wrenching sob had him rush back to her side. "Miss Elizabeth?"

He knelt down in front of her, on one knee, so that he could see at least some part of her countenance. What had caused her distress? He had only stood up to... oh. "Did you think that I had left? That I was departing for Netherfield?"

She nodded. Then a wavering voice came from behind her hands. "You are not?"

Mr. Darcy bit his fist to keep from chuckling out loud. They had to be the two worst conversationalists in all of England, but he knew for a fact that they were not. Just only with each other.

"I suggest Miss Elizabeth, that in the future, we always speak exactly what is on our mind and what we mean without hesitation." Again he bit his fist to stop his chuckling. He could laugh now, as he was filled with euphoria at the knowledge that Elizabeth cared for him strongly.

A grin formed into the biggest smile that had ever graced his countenance. She still sat hunched in her chair, her face hidden by her hands. He wanted to reach out, pull her fingers away so that he could see her beautiful eyes. But propriety kept him still. They were not betrothed, yet.

Even though he was quite sure of her response, the thought of asking her tightened the muscles in his back and sped up his heart. He swallowed. "Miss Elizabeth Bennet, will you do me the honor of being my wife?"

SHE DID NOT BREATHE for she thought she had heard... but that was... Elizabeth lowered her hands and lifted her head to study Mr. Darcy's countenance.

He smiled even more broadly.

She swallowed. "I... excuse me, but I thought you just asked..."

"I did."

Elizabeth knew she must look like a ninny with a blotchy face, tears running down her cheeks and mouth open, but her headache-riddled mind had a hard time processing this. He could not have possibly... but he had. She had better answer quickly. "Yes."

Mr. Darcy's grin threatened to burst off his countenance. "You have made me the happiest man in all of England. No, in all the world."

Slowly she grinned, then chuckled. Her grin

grew into a wide smile, and her chuckling turned into laughter.

Mr. Darcy, her betrothed, reached for her hand and stood, pulling her up with him. He laughed with her and held her with his arms wrapped around her back. Her tears were now due to extraordinary happiness.

Mrs. Bennet cried out as she rushed towards them. "Another one betrothed! I told you, Lizzy, that you need only stay here and you would find a man to marry and I was right."

Elizabeth groaned into Mr. Darcy's chest. He squeezed her, then stepped back, removing his arms but grabbing her hand to hold.

Mr. and Mrs. Bennet stood near with beaming smiles. Her father shook Mr. Darcy's hand while her mother hugged her tightly.

Mrs. Bennet whispered in her ear. "Think of all the dresses, carriages, and clothes you shall have! Oh and your wedding trousseau! I must find out the best houses."

Elizabeth pulled back with a smile, then reached for his hand again. She looked up at him, and he looked at her smiling, then squeezed her hand.

"What is all the commotion?" Lydia walked into the room then stopped and stared.

"Lydia," cried Mrs. Bennet. "Wish your sister glad tidings! Mr. Darcy just asked Elizabeth to marry him!"

Elizabeth barely shook her head and glanced at her betrothed with a smile. His lips were turned up as he lovingly gazed at her. She beamed even more.

Lydia walked over to them, then stopped, tilting her head. "I congratulate you, sister and Mr. Darcy." She smiled. "Now, you have to thank me, as it was due to my going to Brighton that you saw each other again."

Elizabeth turned to Mr. Darcy with big eyes. How fast could they get married?

The End.

ALSO BY BELLA BREEN

The Poison Series

Pride and Prejudice and Poison Book 1

Elizabeth suddenly falls ill after Lady Catherine's unexpected visit...

Pride and Prejudice and Secrets Book 2

Just when Elizabeth thought the danger was over...

Standalone Stories

Forced to Marry

Forced to marry...even though they hate each other.

The Rescue of Elizabeth Bennet

Elizabeth will marry Mr. Collins even if Mrs. Bennet has to drag her to the altar.

Love Unmasked

Is Mr. Darcy Too Late?

Mr. Darcy Goes to Brighton

An Unexpected Second Chance...But Will Lydia ruin it?

Four Months to Wed

An epidemic. A forced marriage. Can love bloom?

Boxed Set

Join the mailing list to get notified when chapters of works in progress are posted!

Bella Breen's Facebook

If you enjoyed the story I hope you'll consider leaving a review. Reviews are vital to any author's career, and I would be extremely thankful and appreciative if you'd consider writing one for me.

Would you like a free Pride and Prejudice cross stitch pattern I created? It's the most loved quote from the book. Download it for free from the file section of https://www.facebook.com/groups/prideandprejudicevariations/

Will you join me for the next book? Follow along as I write at www.bellabreen.com.

Made in the USA
Monee, IL
24 January 2020